APPOINTMENT AT THE DEATH STAR

The star ahead continued to brighten, its glow evidently coming from within. It assumed a circular outline.

As they drew nearer, craters and mountains gradually became visible. Yet there was something extremely odd about them. The craters were far too regular in outline, the mountains far too vertical.

'That's no moon,' Kenobi said softly, 'that's a space station. Let's get out of here!'

Gauges began to whine in protest and by ones and twos every instrument on the control console went berserk. Try as they might they couldn't keep the surface of the gargantuan station from looming steadily larger.

The true size of the battle station became apparent as the freighter was pulled closer and closer. Now only a miniscule speck against the grey bulk of the station, the *Millennium Falcon* was sucked toward one of these steel pseudopods and was instantly swallowed up.

A lake of metal closed off the entryway and the freighter vanished as if it had never existed . . .

STAR WARS

Starring

Mark Hamill **Harrison Ford** **Carrie Fisher**

Peter Cushing

and

Alec Guinness

with

Anthony Daniels **Kenny Baker**
Peter Mayhew and **Dave Prowse**

Written and Directed by
George Lucas

Produced by
Gary Kurtz

Production Designer —————— **John Barry**
Director of Photography —————— **Gil Taylor**
Music by —————————————— **John Williams**

Special Visual Effects Supervisors:
Miniatures & Optical Effects ——————
John Dykstra
Production & Mechanical Effects ——————
John Stears

Film Editors —————————— **Marcia Lucas**
Richard Chew
Paul Hirsch

A Lucasfilm Ltd. Production
A Twentieth Century-Fox Release
Panavision®
Technicolor®
Prints by Deluxe®

Making Films Sound Better

 DOLBY SYSTEM ®
Noise Reduction—High Fidelity

Star Wars
From the Adventures of Luke Skywalker

A Novel by
GEORGE LUCAS

SPHERE BOOKS LIMITED
30/32 Gray's Inn Road, London WC1X 8JL

First full-length edition published in Great Britain by
Sphere Books Ltd 1977
This abridgement published by
Sphere Books Ltd, 1978
Copyright © 1976, 1978 by The Star Wars Corporation
Published by arrangement with Ballantine Books,
a division of Random House, Inc., New York.

TRADE
MARK

Set in Intertype Times

Printed in Great Britain by
Hunt Barnard Printing Ltd.,
Aylesbury, Bucks.

PROLOGUE

Another galaxy, another time.

The Old Republic was the Republic of legend, greater than distance or time. Once, under the wise rule of the Senate and the protection of the Jedi Knights, the Republic throve and grew. But as often happens, then appear those evil ones who have greed to match. The Republic rotted from within.

Aided and abetted by restless, power-hungry individuals, the ambitious Senator Palpatine caused himself to be elected President of the Republic. He promised to reunite the people and to restore the glory of the Republic.

Once in office he declared himself Emperor, shutting himself away from the populace. Soon he was controlled by the very assistants and boot-lickers he had appointed to high office, and the cries of the people for justice did not reach his ears.

Having exterminated the Jedi Knights, the Imperial governors and bureaucrats prepared to institute a reign of terror. Many used the imperial forces and the name of the isolated Emperor to further their own ambitions.

But a small number of systems rebelled at these outrages. Declaring themselves opposed to the New Order they began the great battle to restore the Old Republic.

From the beginning they were vastly outnumbered. In those first dark days it seemed certain the bright flame of resistance would be extinguished before it could cast the light of new truth across a galaxy of oppressed and beaten peoples...

From the First Saga
Journal of the Whills

'They were in the wrong place at the wrong time. Naturally they became heroes.'

Leia Organa of Alderaan, Senator

ONE

It was a vast, shining globe. Not until entering close orbit around it, did its discoverers realise that this was a world in a binary system and not a third sun.

At first it seemed certain nothing could exist on such a planet, least of all humans. Yet both massive G1 and G2 stars orbited a common centre with peculiar regularity, and Tatooine circled them far enough out to permit the development of a stable, if hot, climate. Mostly this was a desert of a world, whose starlike yellow glow was the result of double sunlight striking sodium-rich sands and flats. That same sunlight suddenly shone on the thin skin of a metallic shape falling crazily towards the atmosphere.

The erratic course the galactic cruiser was travelling was intentional, not the product of injury but of a desperate desire to avoid it. Long streaks of intense energy slid close past its hulk.

One of those probing, questing beams succeeded in touching the fleeing ship, striking its principal solar fin. Fragments of metal and plastic erupted into space as the end of the fin distintegrated. The vessel seemed to shudder.

The source of those energy beams suddenly hove into view – a lumbering Imperial cruiser, its massive outline bristling with dozens of heavy weapons emplacements. The cruiser moved in close. Intermittent explosions and flashes of light could be seen in those portions of the smaller ship which had taken hits. The cruiser snuggled up alongside its wounded prey.

Another distant explosion shook the ship – but it didn't feel distant to Artoo Detoo or See Threepio. The

7

concussion bounced them around the narrow corridor like bearings in an old motor.

To look at these two, one would have supposed that the tall, human-like machine, Threepio, was the master and the stubby, tripodal robot, Artoo Detoo, an inferior. But they were in fact equal in everything save loquacity. Here Threepio was clearly the superior.

Still another explosion rattled the corridor, throwing Threepio off balance. Artoo glanced up at Threepio, who was steadying himself against a corridor wall. Lights blinked enigmatically around a single mechanical eye as the smaller robot studied the battered casing of his friend. A patina of metal and fibrous dust coated the usually gleaming bronze finish, and there were some visible dents.

Accompanying the last attack was a persistent deep hum. Then for no apparent reason, the thrumming ceased, and the only sounds came from the crackle of shorting relays or the pops of dying circuitry. Explosions began to echo through the ship once more, but they were far away from the corridor.

Threepio turned his smooth, humanlike head to one side. Metallic ears listened intently. The slim robot had been programmed to blend perfectly among human company.

'Did you hear that?' he inquired. 'They've shut down the main reactor and the drive. This time we'll be destroyed for sure.'

Artoo did not comment immediately. The metre-high robot was engrossed in studying the roof overhead. A series of short beeps and chirps issued from his speaker. To Threepio they formed words as clear and pure as direct current.

'I suppose they did have to shut the drive down,' Threepio admitted, 'but what are we going to do now? We can't enter atmosphere with our main stabiliser fin destroyed. I can't believe we're simply going to surrender.'

A small band of armed humans suddenly appeared, rifles held at the ready.

Threepio watched silently until they had vanished around a far bend in the passageway, then looked back at Artoo. Artoo's senses were slightly sharper than his own.

'What is it, Artoo?' A short burst of beeping came in response. For a minute or two more, the corridor remained deathly silent. Then a faint *scrape*, *scrape* could be heard above, produced by heavy footsteps and the movement of bulky equipment on the ship's hull.

Threepio murmured, 'They've broken in somewhere above us. There's no escape for the Captain this time.' Turning, he peered down at Artoo. 'I think we'd better –'

The shriek of overstressed metal filled the air before he could finish, and the far end of the passageway was lit by a blinding flash. The little cluster of armed crew who had passed by minutes before had encountered the ship's attackers.

Threepio turned his face and delicate photoreceptors away – just in time to avoid the fragments of metal that flew down the corridor. At the far end a gaping hole appeared in the roof, and reflective forms like big metal beads began dropping to the corridor floor. Both robots knew that no machine could match the fluidity with which those shapes moved and instantly assumed fighting postures. The new arrivals were humans in armour, not mechanicals.

One of them looked straight at Threepio – no, not at him, the panicked robot thought frantically, but past him. The figure shifted its big rifle around in armoured hands – too late. A beam of intense light struck the head, sending pieces of armour, bone, and flesh flying in all directions.

Half the invading Imperial troops turned and began returning fire up the corridor – aiming past the two robots.

'Quick – this way!' Threepio ordered. Artoo turned

9

with him. They had taken only a couple of steps when they saw the rebel crewmen in position ahead, firing *down* the corridor. In seconds the passageway was filled with smoke and crisscrossing beams of energy.

Red, green and blue bolts ricocheted off polished sections of wall and floor or ripped long gashes in metal surfaces. Screams of injured and dying humans echoed piercingly above the destruction.

One beam struck near the robot's feet. A second one burst the wall directly behind him, exposing sparking circuitry and rows of conduits. The force of the twin blast tumbled Threepio into the shredded cables, where a dozen different currents turned him into a jerking, twisting display.

Smoke began to fill the corridor. Artoo Detoo bustled about trying to help free his friend. He was built so low that most of the beams passed over him.

Threepio yelled, 'I think something is melting. Free my left leg – the trouble's near the pelvic servomotor.' Typically, his tone turned abruptly from pleading to berating.

'This is all your fault!' he shouted angrily. 'I should have – ' Artoo Detoo cut him off in midspeech with some angry beepings, though he continued to cut and pull at the tangled high-voltage cables.

Threepio sneered in reply. 'The same to you, you little . . . !'

An exceptionally violent explosion shook the passage, drowning him out. A miasma of carbonised component filled the air, obscuring everything.

Two metres tall. Bipedal. Flowing black robes trailing from the figure and a face forever masked by a functional if bizarre black metal breath screen – a Dark Lord of the Sith was an awesome, threatening shape as it strode through the corridors of the rebel ship.

Fear followed the footsteps of all the Dark Lords. The cloud of evil which clung tight about this one was intense enough to cause hardened Imperial troops to back away, menacing enough to set them muttering nervously among themselves. Once-resolute rebel crew-members ceased resisting, broke and ran in panic at the sight of the black armour – armour which, though black as it was, was not nearly as dark as the one obsession which dominated that mind now.

Only a robot was left to stir freely in the wake of the Dark Lord's passing. Threepio finally stepped clear of the last restraining cable. Somewhere behind him human screams could be heard from where relentless Imperial troops were mopping up the last remnants of rebel resistance.

Threepio glanced down and saw only scarred deck. As he looked around, his voice was full of concern. 'Artoo Detoo – where are you?'

Artoo Detoo was there. But he wasn't looking in Threepio's direction. Instead, the little robot appeared frozen in an attitude of attention. Leaning over him was a human figure. It was young, slim, and by human standards, of a calm beauty. One small hand seemed to be moving over the front of Artoo's torso.

Threepio started toward them. But when he reached the end of the corridor, only Artoo stood there, waiting.

'Where have you been?' Threepio finally asked. 'Hiding, I suppose.' He decided not to mention the maybe-human.

'They'll be coming back this way,' he went on, nodding down the corridor, 'looking for human survivors. What are we going to do now? We'll be sent to the spice mines of Kessel or taken apart for spare components. That's if they don't consider us potential pro-gramme traps and blow us apart on sight. If we don't . . . ' But Artoo had already turned and was ambling quickly back down the passageway.

'Wait, where are you going? Haven't you been listen-ing to me?' Uttering curses in several languages, Threepio raced fluidly after his friend.

Outside the galactic cruiser's control centre the corridor

was crowded with sullen prisoners gathered by Imperial troops. Some lay wounded, some dying. Several officers had been separated from the enlisted ranks and stood in a small group by themselves.

As if on command, everyone – Imperial troops and rebels – became silent as a massive caped form came from behind a turn in the passage. Two rebel officers began to shake. Stopping before one of the men, the towering figure reached out. A massive hand closed around the man's neck and lifted him off the deck. The rebel officer's eyes bulged, but he kept his silence.

An Imperial officer scrambled down out of the fighter's control room. 'Nothing, sir. Information retrieval system's been wiped clean.'

Darth Vader acknowledged this news with a barely perceptible nod. The impenetrable mask turned to regard the officer. Metal-clad fingers contracted. Reaching up, the prisoner desperately tried to pry them loose, but to no avail.

'Where is the data you intercepted?' Vader rumbled dangerously. 'What have you done with the information tapes?'

'We – intercepted – no information,' the dangling officer gurgled, barely able to breathe. 'This is a . . . councillor vessel . . . Did you not see our . . . exterior markings? We're on a . . . diplomatic . . . mission.'

'Chaos take your mission!' Vader growled. 'Where are those tapes!' He squeezed harder.

The officer's voice was a bare, choked whisper. 'Only . . . the Commander knows.'

'This ship carries the system crest of Alderaan,' Vader growled, the gargoylelike mask leaning close. 'Is any of the royal family on board? Who are you carrying?' Thick fingers tightened further, and the officer's struggles became more and more frantic. His last words were muffled and choked past intelligibility.

Vader was not pleased. Even though the figure went limp, that hand continued to tighten, producing a chilling snapping and popping of bone. Then with a disgusted wheeze Vader finally threw the doll-form of the dead man against a far wall.

The massive form whirled unexpectedly. 'Start tearing this ship apart piece by piece, until you find those tapes. As for passengers, if any, I want them alive.' He paused, then added, '*Quickly!*'

Artoo Detoo finally came to a halt in an empty corridor devoid of smoke and the signs of battle. A worried, confused Threepio pulled up behind him.

'You've led us through half the ship, and to what . . . ?' He broke off, staring in disbelief as the squat robot reached up with one clawed limb and snapped the seal on a lifeboat hatch. Immediately a red warning light came on and a low hooting sounded in the corridor.

Threepio looked wildly in all directions, but the passageway remained empty. When he looked back, Artoo was already working his way into the cramped boat pod. It was large enough to hold several humans, not laid out to accommodate mechanicals. Artoo had some trouble negotiating the little compartment.

'Hey,' a startled Threepio called, 'you're not permitted in there! It's restricted to humans. We just might be able to convince the Imperials that we're too valuable to break up, but if someone sees you in there we haven't a chance. Come on out.'

Somehow Artoo had succeeded in wedging his body into position in front of the miniature control board. He cocked his body slightly and threw a stream of loud beeps.

Threepio listened. 'Mission . . . what mission? You sound like you haven't got an integrated logic terminal left in your brain. No . . . no more adventures. I'm *not* getting in there. I'll take my chances with the Imperials.'

An angry electronic twang came from the Artoo unit.

Threepio was concocting a rejoinder when an explosion blew out the back wall of the corridor. Flames

13

began jumping hungrily from the exposed interior wall.

The lanky robot jumped into the life pod. 'I'm going to regret this,' he muttered as Artoo activated the safety door behind him. The smaller robot flipped a series of switches, snapped back a cover, and pressed three buttons in a certain sequence. With the thunder of explosive latches the life pod ejected from the crippled fighter.

When word came that the last pocket of resistance on the rebel ship had been cleaned out, the Captain of the Imperial cruiser relaxed. He was listening with pleasure to the proceedings on the captured vessel when one of his chief gunnery officers called to him. Moving to the man's position, the Captain stared into the circular viewscreen and saw a tiny dot dropping away towards the fiery world below.

'There goes another pod, sir. Instructions?' The officer's hand hovered over a computerised energy battery.

Casually, the Captain studied the nearby readouts monitoring the pod. All of them read blank.

'Hold your fire, Lieutenant Hija. Instruments show no life forms aboard. The pod's release mechanism must have short-circuited or received a false instruction. Don't waste your power.'

Glare from exploding panels and erupting circuitry reflected crazily off the armour of the lead storm trooper as he surveyed the passageway ahead. He was about to call for those behind to follow him when he noticed something crouching back in a small, dark alcove. Holding his pistol ready, he moved cautiously forward.

A small, shivering figure clad in flowing white hugged the back of the recess and stared up at the man. He faced a young woman, and her physical description fit that of the individual the Dark Lord was most interested in. The trooper grinned behind his helmet. He would be commended.

Within the armour his head turned slightly, directing his voice to the tiny condenser microphone. 'Here she is,' he called.

Once his attention turned from the girl to his communicator her shivering vanished with startling speed. The energy pistol she had held out of sight came up and around as she burst from her hiding place.

The trooper who found her fell, his head a mass of melted bone and metal. The same fate met the second armoured form coming up fast behind him. Then a bright green energy pole touched the woman's side and she slumped to the deck, the pistol still locked in her small palm.

Metal-encased shapes clustered around her. One lower officer knelt and turned her over. He studied the paralysed form with a practised eye.

'She'll be all right,' he finally declared. 'Report to Lord Vader.'

Threepio stared out the small viewport set in the front of the escape pod as the hot yellow eye of Tatooine began to swallow them up. Behind them, the crippled fighter and the Imperial cruiser were receding to imperceptibility.

Artoo's seemingly random manipulation of the pod controls promised anything but a smooth landing, however. Threepio regarded his squat companion with concern.

'Are you sure you know how to pilot this thing?'

TWO

It was an old settlers' saying that you could burn your eyes out faster by staring at the sun-scorched flatlands of Tatooine than by looking directly at its two huge suns. Yet despite the glare, life did exist in the flatlands formed by long-evaporated seabeds. One thing made it possible: the reintroduction of water.

For human purposes, the water of Tatooine was only marginally accessible. The atmosphere yielded its moisture with reluctance. It had to be coaxed, forced, yanked out of the hard blue sky to the parched surface.

Two figures whose concern was obtaining that moisture were standing on a slight rise of one of those inhospitable flats. One was stiff and metallic – a sand-pitted vaporator sunk securely through sand into deeper rock. The figure next to it was a good deal more animated, though no less sun-weathered.

Luke Skywalker was twice the age of the ten-year-old vaporator. At the moment he was swearing softly at a recalcitrant valve adjuster on the device. From time to time he resorted to some unsubtle pounding in place of using the appropriate tool. Neither method worked very well.

As Luke considered his predicament, a third figure appeared, scooting out from behind the vaporator to fumble awkwardly at the damaged section. Only three of the Treadwell model robot's six arms were functioning, and these had seen much wear. The machine moved with unsteady, stop-and-start motions.

Luke gazed at it sadly, then inclined his head to study the sky. Still no sign of a cloud, and he knew there never would be unless he got that vaporator working. He was about to try once again when a small, intense gleam of light caught his eye. Quickly he slipped the carefully cleaned set of macro-binoculars from his belt and focused the lenses skyward.

As he stared, the day's chores were forgotten. Clipping the binoculars back on to his belt, Luke turned and dashed for the landspeeder. Half-way to the vehicle he thought to call behind him.

'Hurry up,' he shouted impatiently. 'What are you waiting for? Get it in gear.'

The Treadwell started towards him, hesitated, and then commenced spinning in a tight circle, smoke belching from every joint. Luke shouted further instructions, then gave up in disgust when he realised that it would take more than words to motivate the Treadwell again.

Luke gunned the engine, which whined in protest, and sand erupted behind the floater as he aimed the craft towards the distant town of Anchorhead.

Behind him, a pitiful beacon of black smoke from the burning robot continued to rise into the clear desert air. It wouldn't be there when Luke returned. There were scavengers of metal as well as flesh in the wide wastes of Tatooine.

Metal and stone structures bleached white by the glaze of twin Tatoo I and II huddled together tightly, for company as much as for protection. They formed the nexus of the widespread farming community of Anchorhead.

Presently the dusty, unpaved streets were quiet, deserted. A lone old woman appeared and started across the street. Her metallic sun shawl was pulled tight around her.

Panting and waving an angry fist after the landspeeder, she raised her voice over the sound of its passage. 'Won't you kids ever learn to slow down!'

Luke didn't hear her. His attention was focused elsewhere as he pulled up behind a low, long concrete station.

Luke slammed the front door aside. 'Hey, every-body!'

He ran towards the instrument room at the rear of the station.

Deak and Windy looked up from the computer-assisted pool game as Luke burst into the room. They were dressed much like Luke.

All three youths contrasted strikingly with the burly, handsome player at the far side of the table, with his clipped hair and his precision-cut uniform. Behind the three humans a soft hum came from a repair robot who was working patiently on a broken piece of station equipment.

'Shape it up, you guys,' Luke yelled excitedly. Then he noticed the older man in the uniform. 'Biggs!'

The man's face twisted in a half grin. 'Hello, Luke.' Then they were embracing each other warmly.

Luke finally stood away, openly admiring the uniform. 'I didn't know you were back. When did you get in?'

'Just a little while ago. I wanted to surprise you, hot-shot.' He indicated the room. 'I thought you'd be here with these other two nightcrawlers.' Deak and Windy both smiled. 'I certainly didn't expect you to be out working.' He laughed easily.

'The academy didn't change you much,' Luke commented. 'But you're back so soon.' His expression grew concerned. 'Hey, what happened – didn't you get your commission?'

There was something evasive about Biggs as he re-plied. 'Of course I got it. Signed to serve aboard the freighter *Rand Ecliptic* just last week. First Mate Biggs Darklighter, at your service. 'I just came back to say good-bye to you unfortunate landlocked simpletons.' They all laughed, until Luke suddenly remembered what had brought him here in such a hurry.

'There's a battle going on right here in our system. Come and look,' he told them, his initial excitement returning.

Deak looked disappointed. 'Not another one of your epic battles, Luke. Haven't you dreamed up enough of them?'

'I'm serious. It's a battle, all right.'

With words and shoves he managed to cajole the occupants of the station out into the strong sunlight.

Luke already had his macrobinoculars out and was searching the heavens. It took only a moment for him to fix on a particular spot. 'I told you,' he insisted. 'There they are.'

Biggs moved alongside him and reached for the binoculars as the others strained unaided eyes. A slight readjustment provided enough magnification for Biggs to make out two silvery specks against the dark blue.

'That's no battle, hotshot,' he decided, lowering the binocs. 'They're just sitting there. Two ships, all right – probably a barge loading a freighter, since Tatooine hasn't got an orbital station.'

'There was a lot of firing – earlier,' Luke added. His initial enthusiasm was beginning to falter.

'I keep telling you, Luke,' the mechanic said, with the air of a man tired of repeating the same story, 'the rebellion is a long way from here. I doubt if the Empire would fight to keep this system, Tatooine is a big hunk of nothing.'

His audience began to fade back into the station before Luke could mutter a reply. He followed them, but not without a last glance back and up to the distant specks. One thing he was sure of were the flashes of light he had seen between the two ships. They hadn't been caused by the suns of Tatooine reflecting off metal.

The binding that locked the girl's hands behind her back was primitive and effective. The constant attention the squad of heavily armed troopers might have been out of place for one small female, but their lives depended on her being delivered safely.

When she deliberately slowed her pace, her captors did not mind mistreating her. One of the armoured figures shoved her brutally in the small of the back, and she nearly fell. Turning, she gave the offending soldier a vicious look.

The hallway they eventually emerged into was still smoking around the edges of the smouldering cavity blasted through the hull of the fighter. A portable accessway had been sealed to it, bridging space between the rebel craft and the cruiser. A shadow moved over her as she turned from inspecting the accessway.

Above her towered the threatening bulk of Darth Vader, red eyes glaring behind the hideous mask. A muscle twitched in one smooth cheek, but other than that the girl didn't react. Nor was there the slightest shake in her voice.

'Darth Vader . . . I should have known. Only you would be so bold – and so stupid. Well, the Imperial Senate will not sit still for this. When they hear that you have attacked a diplomatic miss –'

'Senator Leia Organa,' Vader rumbled softly. 'You aren't on any mercy mission this time. You passed directly through a restricted system, ignoring numerous warnings and completely disregarding orders to turn about.'

The huge metal skull dipped close. 'I know that several transmissions were beamed to this vessel by spies within that system. When we traced those transmissions back to the individuals with whom they originated, they had the poor grace to kill themselves before they could be questioned. I want to know what happened to the data they sent you.'

Neither Vader's words nor presence had any effect on the girl. 'I don't know what you're blathering about,' she snapped, looking away from him. 'I'm a member of the Senate on a diplomatic mission to –'

'To your part of the rebel alliance,' Vader declared, cutting her off accusingly. 'You're also a traitor.' His gaze went to a nearby officer. 'Take her away.'

She succeeded in reaching him with her spit, which hissed against still-hot battle armour. He wiped the offensive matter away, watching her with interest as she was marched through the accessway into the cruiser.

A tall, slim soldier attracted Vader's attention as he came up next to him. 'Holding her is dangerous,' he ventured. 'If word of this does get out, there will be much unrest in the Senate. It will generate sympathy for the rebels.' The Commander looked up at the unreadable metal face, then added. 'She should be destroyed immediately.'

'No. My first duty is to locate that hidden fortress of theirs,' Vader replied. 'She is now my only key to discovering its location. I intend to make full use of her.'

The Commander pursed his lips. 'She'll die before she gives you any information.'

Vader's reply was chilling in its indifference. 'Leave that to me.' He then went on. 'Send out a wide-band distress signal. Indicate that the Senator's ship encountered an unexpected meteorite cluster it could not avoid. Inform her father and the Senate that all aboard were killed.'

A cluster of tired-looking troops marched purposefully up to their Commander and the Dark Lord. Vader eyed them expectantly.

'The data tapes are not aboard the ship. There is no valuable information in the ship's storage banks and no evidence of bank erasure,' the officer in charge recited. 'Nor were any transmissions directed outward from the ship from the time we made contact. A malfunctioning lifeboat pod was ejected during the fighting, but it was confirmed that no life forms were on board.'

Vader appeared thoughtful. 'It might have contained the tapes. Tapes are not life forms. In all probability any native finding them would be ignorant of their importance and would likely clear them for his own use. Still . . .

'Send down a detachment to retrieve them, or to make certain they are not in the pod,' he finally ordered.

'Be subtle; there is no need to attract attention, even on this miserable outpost world.'

Vader turned his gaze back to the Commander. 'Vaporise this fighter – we don't want to leave anything. As for the pod, I cannot take the chance it was a simple malfunction. The data it might contain could prove too damaging. See to this personally, Commander. If those data tapes exist, they must be retrieved or destroyed at all costs.' Then he added with satisfaction, 'With that accomplished and the Senator in our hands, we will see the end of this absurd rebellion.'

'What a forsaken place this is!'

Threepio turned cautiously to look back at the pod, half buried in sand. His internal gyros were still unsteady from the rough landing.

A faint cloud of minute dust particles rose in their wake as the two robots marched away. Neither had been designed for pedal locomotion on this kind of terrain, so they had to fight their way across the unstable surface.

Threepio paused, but Artoo Detoo did not. The little automaton had performed a sharp turn and was now ambling slowly but steadily in the direction of the nearest outjut of mesa.

'Where do you think you're going?' Threepio yelled.

Artoo paused, emitting a stream of electronic explanation.

'Well, I'm not going that way,' Threepio declared. 'It's too rocky.' He gestured, at an angle away from the cliffs. 'This way is much easier.' A metal hand waved disparagingly at the high mesas. 'What makes you think there are any settlements that way, anyhow?'

A long whistle issued from the depths of Artoo.

'All right, go your way,' Threepio announced grandly. 'You'll be sandlogged within a day, you nearsighted scrap pile.' He gave the Artoo unit a contemptuous shove, sending the smaller robot tumbling down a slight dune. As it struggled at the bottom to regain its feet,

22

Threepio started off towards the blurred, glaring horizon, glancing back over his shoulder. 'Don't let me catch you following me, begging for help,' he warned, 'because you won't get it.'

Several hours later a straining Threepio, his internal thermostat overloaded and edging dangerously towards overheat shutdown, struggled to the top of what he hoped was the last towering dune, and peered anxiously ahead. Instead of the hoped-for greenery of human civilisation he saw only several dozen more dunes. The farthest rose even higher.

He could continue on his present course, he told himself. Or he could confess to an error in judgement and try to catch up again with Artoo Detoo. Neither prospect held much appeal for him.

Already his receptors were beginning to go. He saw something moving in the distance. It was definitely light on metal, and it was moving towards him. His hopes soared. He rose and began waving frantically.

It was, he saw now, definitely a vehicle, though of a type unfamiliar to him. But it implied intelligence and technology.

Luke and Biggs were walking in the shade outside the power-station.

'Luke, I didn't come back just to say good-bye, or to crow over everyone because I got through the Academy.' Biggs seemed to hesitate, unsure of himself. Then he blurted out rapidly, 'I want somebody to know. I can't tell my parents.'

Gaping, Luke could only gulp, 'Know what?'

'About the talking that's been going on at the Academy – and other places, Luke. I made some new friends, outsystem friends. We agreed about the way certain things are developing, and – ' his voice dropped conspiratorially – 'When we reach one of the peripheral systems, we're going to jump ship and join the Alliance.'

Luke stared back at his friend, tried to picture fun-loving, happy-go-lucky Biggs as a patriot afire with rebellious fervour.

'You're going to join the rebellion?' he started. 'You've got to be kidding. How?'

Biggs continued, 'A friend of mine from the Academy has a friend on Bestine who might enable us to make contact with an armed rebel unit.'

'You're crazy,' Luke announced with conviction. If rebel outposts were so easy to find, the Empire would have wiped them out years ago.'

'I know it's a long shot,' Biggs admitted. 'If I don't contact them, then I'll do what I can, on my own.'

He stared intensely at his friend. 'Luke, the rebellion is spreading. And I want to be on the right side – the side I believe in.' His voice altered unpleasantly. 'You should have heard some of the stories I've heard, Luke, learned of some of the outrages. The Empire may have been great and beautiful once, but the people in charge now – ' He shook his head sharply. 'It's rotten, Luke, rotten.'

'And I can't do a damn thing,' Luke muttered morosely. 'I'm stuck here.'

'I thought you were going to enter the Academy soon,' Biggs observed. 'Then you'll have your chance to get off this sandpile.'

Luke snorted derisively. 'I had to withdraw my application.' He looked away, unable to meet his friend's disbelieving stare. 'There's been a lot of unrest among the sandpeople since you left, Biggs. They've even raided the outskirts of Anchorhead.'

Biggs shook his head, disregarding the excuse. 'Your uncle could hold off a whole colony of raiders with one blaster.'

'From the house, sure,' Luke agreed, 'but Uncle Owen's finally got enough vaporators installed and running to make the farm pay off big. But he can't guard all that land by himself. He needs me for one more season.'

Biggs sighed sadly. 'What good is all your uncle's work if it's taken over by the Empire? I've heard that they're starting to imperialise commerce in all the outlying systems. It won't be long before your uncle and everyone else on Tatooine are just tenants slaving for the greater glory of the Empire.'

'That couldn't happen here,' Luke objected with a confidence he didn't quite feel. 'You've said it yourself – the Empire won't bother with this rock.'

'Things change, Luke. Only the threat of rebellion keeps many in power from doing certain unmentionable things. If that threat is completely removed – well, there are two things men have never been able to satisfy: their curiosity and their greed.'

Both men stood silent.

'I wish I was going with you,' Luke finally murmured. 'Will you be around long?'

'No. I'm leaving in the morning to rendezvous with the *Ecliptic*.'

'Then I guess . . . I won't be seeing you again.'

'Maybe someday,' Biggs declared. 'I'll keep a look out for you, hotshot.'

'I'll be at the Academy the season after,' Luke insisted. 'After that, who knows where I'll end up?' He sounded determined. 'I won't be drafted into the starfleet, that's for sure. Take care of yourself. You'll . . . always be the best friend I've got.'

'So long, then, Luke,' Biggs said simply. He turned and re-entered the power station.

Luke watched him disappear through the door, his own thoughts as chaotic as one of Tatooine's dust storms.

There were any number of extraordinary features unique to Tatooine's surface. Outstanding among them were the mysterious mists which rose regularly from the ground at the points where desert sands washed up against unyielding cliffs and mesas.

Neither the mist nor the alien moans of nocturnal desert dwellers troubled Artoo Detoo, as he made his careful way up the rocky arroyo, hunting for the easiest pathway to the mesa top. His squarish, broad footpads made loud clicking sounds as sand underfoot gave way gradually to gravel.

For a moment, he paused. He seemed to detect a noise – like metal on rock – ahead of him. The sound wasn't repeated, and he quickly resumed his ambling ascent.

Up the arroyo, too far up to be seen from below, a pebble trickled loose from the stone wall. The tiny figure which had accidentally dislodged the pebble retreated mouselike into shadow. Two glowing points of light showed under overlapping folds of brown cape a metre from the narrowing canyon wall.

Only the reaction of the unsuspecting robot indicated the presence of the whining beam as it struck him. For a moment Artoo Detoo fluoresced eerily in the dimming light. There was a single short electronic squeak. Then the tripodal support unbalanced and the tiny automaton toppled on to its back, the lights on its front blinking on and off erratically.

Three travesties of men scurried out from behind boulders. Their motions were more of rodent than human, and they stood little taller than the Artoo unit. When they saw that the single burst of enervating energy had immobilised the robot, they holstered their peculiar weapons. Nevertheless, they approached the machine cautiously.

Unhealthy red-yellow pupils glowed catlike from the depths of their hoods as they studied their captive. The jawas conversed in low guttural croaks and scrambled analogues of human speech. If they had ever been human, they had long since degenerated past anything resembling the human race.

Several more jawas appeared. They succeeded in alternately hoisting and dragging the robot back down the arroyo.

At the bottom – like some monstrous prehistoric beast – was a sandcrawler as enormous as its operators were tiny. Several dozen metres high, the vehicle towered above the ground on multiple treads that were taller than a man. Its metal epidermis was battered and pitted from withstanding untold sandstorms.

On reaching the crawler, the jawas resumed jabbering among themselves. Artoo Detoo could hear them but failed to comprehend anything. If they so wished, only jawas could understand other jawas.

One of them removed a small disc from a belt pouch and sealed it to the Artoo unit's flank. A large tube protruded from one side of the gargantuan vehicle. There was a brief moan, the *whoosh* of powerful vacuum, and the small robot was sucked into the bowels of the sand-crawler. This part of the job completed, the jawas engaged in another bout of jabbering, then scurried into the crawler via tubes and ladders, like a nest of mice returning to their holes.

None too gently, the suction tube deposited Artoo in a small cubicle. In addition to piles of broken instruments and scrap, a dozen or so robots of differing shapes and sizes populated the prison. A few were locked in electronic conversation. Others muddled aimlessly about. But when Artoo tumbled into the chamber, one voice burst out in surprise.

'Artoo Detoo – it's you!' called an excited Threepio from the near darkness. He made his way over to the still immobilised repair unit. Spotting the small disc sealed on to Artoo's side, Threepio turned his gaze thoughtfully down to his own chest, where a similar device had been attached.

Massive gears, poorly lubricated, started to move. With a groaning and grinding, the monster sandcrawler turned and lumbered into the desert night.

THREE

The conference table was as soulless and unyielding as the mood of the eight Imperial Senators and officers ranged around it. One of the youngest of the eight was declaiming. He exhibited the attitude of one who had climbed fast by methods best not examined too closely. General Tagge did possess a certain twisted genius, but it was only partly that ability which had lifted him to his present exalted position. Many respected him. Or feared him.

'He's gone too far this time,' the General was insisting vehemently. 'This Sith Lord inflicted on us by the Emperor will be our undoing. Until the battle station is fully operational, we remain vulnerable.

'Some of you still don't realise how well equipped and organised the rebel Alliance is. Their vessels are excellent, their pilots better. And they are propelled by something more powerful than mere engines: this perverse, reactionary fanaticism of theirs.'

An older officer, with facial scars so deeply engraved that even the best cosmetic surgery could not repair them, shifted nervously in his chair. 'Dangerous to your starfleet, General Tagge, but not to this battle station.' Wizened eyes hopped from man to man. 'I think Lord Vader knows what he's doing. The rebellion will continue only as long as those cowards have a sanctuary, a place where their pilots can relax and their machines can be repaired.'

Tagge objected. 'I beg to differ with you, Romodi. I think the construction of this station has more to do with Governor Tarkin's bid for personal power than with any justifiable military strategy. Within the Senate the rebels will continue to increase their support as long –'

28

The sound of the single doorway sliding aside and the guard snapping to attention cut him off. His head turned as did everyone else's.

Two individuals as different in appearance as they were united in objectives had entered the chamber. The nearest to Tagge was a thin, hatchet-faced man with the expression of a quiescent piranha. The Grand Moff Tarkin, Governor of numerous outlying Imperial territories, was dwarfed by the broad, armoured bulk of Lord Darth Vader.

Tagge, unintimidated but subdued, slowly resumed his seat as Tarkin assumed his place at the end of the table. Vader stood next to him, a dominating presence behind the Governor's chair. For a minute Tarkin stared directly at Tagge, then glanced away as if he had seen nothing. Tagge fumed but remained silent.

As Tarkin's gaze roved around the table a razor-thin smile of satisfaction remained frozen in his features. 'Gentlemen. I have just received word that the Emperor has permanently dissolved the Imperial Senate. The past remnants of the Old Republic have finally been swept away.'

'This is impossible,' Tagge interjected. 'How will the Emperor maintain control of the Imperial bureaucracy?'

'Senatorial representation has not been formally abolished,' Tarkin explained. 'It has merely been superseded for the duration of the emergency. Regional Governors will now have direct control of their territories. The Imperial presence can at last be brought to bear properly on the vacillating worlds of the Empire. From now on, fear will keep potentially traitorous local governments in line. Fear of the Imperial fleet – and fear of this battle station.'

'And what of the existing rebellion?' Tagge wanted to know.

'If the rebels somehow managed to gain access to a complete technical schema of this battle station, it is remotely possible that they might be able to locate a minor weakness susceptible to exploitation.' Tarkin's smile shifted to a smirk. 'Of course, we all know how well guarded such vital data is. It could not possibly fall into rebel hands.'

'The technical data to which you are obliquely referring,' rumbled Darth Vader angrily, 'will soon be back in our hands. If –'

Tarkin shook the Dark Lord off, something no one else at the table would have dared to do. 'It is immaterial. Any attack made against this station by the rebels would be a suicidal gesture – regardless of any information they managed to obtain. After many long years of secret construction, this station has become the decisive force in this part of the universe. Events in this region of the galaxy will be decided by this station!'

A huge metal-clad hand gestured slightly, and the Dark Lord continued. 'Don't become too proud of this technological terror you've spawned, Tarkin. The ability to destroy a city, a world, a whole system is still insignificant when set against the force.'

' "The Force," ' Tagge sneered. 'Don't try to frighten *us* with your sorcerer's ways, Lord Vader. Your sad devotion to that ancient mythology has not helped you to conjure up those stolen tapes, or to locate the rebels' hidden fortress. Why, it's enough to make one laugh fit to –'

Tagge's eyes abruptly bulged and his hands went to his throat as he began to turn a disconcerting shade of blue.

'I find,' Vader ventured, 'this lack of faith disturbing.'

'Enough of this,' Tarkin snapped. 'Vader, release him. This bickering among ourselves is pointless.'

Vader shrugged. Tagge slumped in his seat, rubbing his throat, his wary gaze never leaving the dark giant.

'Lord Vader will provide us with the location of the rebel fortress by the time this station is certified operational,' Tarkin declared. 'We will proceed to it and destroy it utterly, crushing this pathetic rebellion in one swift stroke.'

'As the Emperor wills it,' Vader added, not without sarcasm, 'so shall it be.'

Threepio endured the discomfiting atmosphere as best he could. It was a constant battle to avoid being thrown by every unexpected bounce into the walls or into a fellow machine.

Then, quite without warning, the sandcrawler's whine died, and the vehicle came to a halt. A nervous buzz rose from those mechanicals who still retained a semblance of sentience as they speculated on their location and probable fate.

Threepio was no longer ignorant of his captors or their likely motives. Local captives had explained the nature of the jawas. Travelling in their enormous mobile fortress-homes, they scoured Tatooine in search of valuable minerals – and salvageable machinery. They had never been seen outside of their protective cloaks and sandmasks, so no one knew exactly what they looked like. But they were reputed to be extraordinarily ugly.

Leaning over his still-motionless companion, he began a steady shaking of the barrel-like torso. 'Wake up,' Threepio urged. 'We've stopped.' Like several of the other, more imaginative robots, his eyes were warily scanning metal walls.

Abruptly the far wall of the chamber slid aside and the blinding white glare of a Tatooine morning rushed in on them. Several repulsive-looking jawas scrambled agilely into the chamber. Using hand weapons of an unknown design, they prodded at the machines. Certain of them did not stir.

Ignoring the immobile ones, the jawas herded those still capable of movement outside, Artoo and Threepio among them. Both robots found themselves part of an uneven line.

Shielding his eyes against the glare, Threepio saw that five of them were arranged alongside the huge sandcrawler. He studied the small domes and vaporators that indicated the presence of a larger underground human homestead. All signs pointed to a modest, if isolated, habitation. His spirits rose correspondingly.

'If we can convince these bipedal vermin to unload us here, we may enter into sensible human service again instead of being melted into slag,' he murmured.

Artoo's reply was a noncommittal chirp. Both machines became silent as the jawas scurried around them, striving to straighten one poor machine with a badly bent spine, to disguise a dent or scrape with liquid and dust.

As two of them bustled about, working on his sand-coated skin, Threepio fought to stifle an expression of disgust. One of his many human-analogue functions was the ability to react naturally to offensive odours. Small insects drifted in clouds about the faces of the jawas, who ignored them.

So intent was Threepio on his observation that he failed to notice the two figures moving towards them from the region of the largest dome. Artoo had to nudge him before he looked up.

The first man wore an air of exhaustion, sandblasted into his face by too many years of arguing with a hostile environment. But his body was still powerful.

Dwarfed by his uncle's wrestlerlike body, Luke strode slump-shouldered in his shadow, his present attitude one of dejection rather than exhaustion.

The bigger man stopped before the assembly and entered into a peculiar squeaky dialogue with the jawa in charge. When they wished it, the jawas could be understood.

Luke stood nearby, listening indifferently. Then he shuffled along behind his uncle as the latter began inspecting the five machines, pausing only to mutter an occasional word or two to his nephew. It was hard to pay attention, even though he knew he ought to be learning.

'Luke – oh, Luke!' a voice called.

Luke walked over to the near edge of the subterranean courtyard and peered down.

A stout woman was busy working among decorative plants. She looked up at him. 'Be sure and tell Owen that if he buys a translator to make sure it speaks Bocce.'

Turning, Luke looked back over his shoulder and studied the motley collection of tired machines. 'It looks like we don't have much of a choice,' he called back to her, 'but I'll remind him anyway.'

Owen Lars had already come to a decision, having settled on a small semi-agricultural robot, similar in shape to Artoo Detoo, save that its multiple subsidiary arms were tipped with different functions. At an order, it had stepped out of the line and was wobbling along behind Owen and the jawa.

Proceeding to the end of the line, the farmer's eyes narrowed as he concentrated on the sand-scoured but still flashy bronze finish of the tall, humanoid Threepio.

'I presume you function,' he grumbled at the robot. 'I need a 'droid that knows something about the binary language of independently programmable moisture vaporators.'

'Vaporators! We are both in luck,' Threepio countered. 'My first post-primary assignment was in programming binary load lifters. Very similar in construction and memory-function to your vaporators. You could almost say . . . .'

Luke tapped his uncle on the shoulder and whispered something in his ear. His uncle nodded, then looked back at Threepio again.

'Do you speak Bocce?'

'Of course, sir,' Threepio replied. 'It's like a second language to me. I'm as fluent in Bocce as – '

The farmer appeared determined never to allow him to conclude a sentence. 'Shut up.' Owen Lars looked down at the jawa. 'I'll take this one, too.'

'Take them down to the garage, Luke,' his uncle instructed him. 'I want you to have both of them cleaned up by suppertime.'

'But I was going into Tosche station to pick up some new power converters and . . .'

'Don't lie to me, Luke,' his uncle warned him. 'I don't mind you wasting time with your idle friends, but only after you've finished your chores. Now hop to it – and before supper, mind.'

Downcast, Luke directed his words irritably to Threepio and the small agricultural robot. 'Follow me, you two.' They started for the garage as Owen entered into price negotiations with the jawa.

Other jawas were leading the three remaining machines back into the sandcrawler when something let out an almost pathetic beep. Luke turned to see the Artoo unit breaking formation and starting towards him. It was immediately restrained by a jawa wielding a control device that activated the disc sealed on the machine's front plate.

Luke studied the rebellious 'droid curiously. A minute later, something pinged sharply nearby. Glancing down, Luke saw that a head plate had popped off the agricultural 'droid. A grinding noise was coming from within. Then the machine was throwing internal components all over the sandy ground.

Owen Lars glared down at the nervous jawa. 'What kind of junk are you trying to push on us?'

The jawa responded loudly, indignantly.

Meanwhile, Artoo Detoo had scuttled out of the group of machines being led back towards the mobile fortress.

Tapping Luke gently on the shoulder, Threepio whispered conspiratorially into his ear. 'If I might say so, young sir, that Artoo unit is a real bargain. In top condition. Don't let all the sand and dust deceive you.'

Luke was in the habit of making instant decisions. 'Uncle Owen!' he called.

His uncle glanced quickly at him. Luke gestured towards Artoo Detoo. 'We don't want any trouble. What about swapping this – ' he indicated the burned-out agricultural 'droid – 'for that one?'

34

The older man studied the Artoo unit, then considered the jawas. Though inherently cowards, the tiny desert scavengers *could* be pushed too far. The sandcrawler could flatten the homestead.

Faced with a no-win situation for either side if he pressed too hard, Owen resumed the argument for show's sake before gruffly assenting. The head jawa consented reluctantly to the trade, and both sides breathed a sigh of relief that hostilities had been avoided. While the jawa bowed and whined with impatient greed, Owen paid him off.

Meanwhile, Luke had led the two robots towards an opening in the dry ground. A few seconds later they were striding down a ramp kept clear of drifting sand by electrostatic repellers.

'Don't you ever forget this,' Threepio muttered to Artoo. 'Why I stick my neck out for you, when all you ever bring me is trouble, is beyond my capacity to comprehend.'

The passage widened into the garage, which was cluttered with tools and sections of farming machinery. Near the centre was a large tub, and the aroma drifting from it made Threepio's principal olfactory sensors twitch.

Luke grinned, noting the robot's reaction. 'Yes, it's a lubrication bath.' He eyed the tall bronze robot appraisingly. 'And from the looks of it, you could use about a week's submergence. But we can't afford that so you'll have to settle for an afternoon.' Then Luke turned his attention to Artoo Detoo, walking up to him and flipping open a panel that shielded numerous gauges.

'As for you,' he continued, 'I don't know how you've kept running. It's recharge time for you.' He gestured towards a large power unit.

Artoo Detoo followed Luke's gesture, then beeped once and waddled over to the boxy construction. Finding the proper cord, he automatically flipped open a panel and plugged the triple prongs into his face.

Threepio had walked over to the large cistern, which was filled with aromatic cleansing oil. With a remarkably humanlike sigh he lowered himself slowly into the tank.

'You two behave yourselves,' Luke cautioned them as he moved to a small two-man skyhopper. 'I've got work of my own to do.'

Unfortunately, Luke's energies were still focused on his farewell encounter with Biggs, so that hours later he had finished few of his chores.

Abruptly something came to a boil within him. He threw a power wrench across a worktable nearby. 'It just isn't fair!' he declared to no one in particular. His voice dropped disconsolately. 'Biggs is right. I'll never get out of here. He's planning rebellion against the Empire, and I'm trapped on a blight of a farm.'

'I beg your pardon, sir.'

Luke spun, startled, but it was only the tall 'droid, Threepio. Bronze-coloured alloy gleamed in the overhead lights of the garage, cleaned of pits and dust by the powerful oils. 'Is there anything I might do to help?' the robot asked solicitously.

Luke studied the machine, and some of his anger drained away. 'I doubt it,' he replied, 'unless you can alter time and speed up the harvest. Or else teleport me off this sandpile under Uncle Owen's nose.'

Threepio considered the question objectively before finally replying, 'I don't think so, sir. I'm only a third-degree 'droid and not very knowledgeable about such things as transatomic physics.' Suddenly, the events of the past couple of days seemed to catch up with him. 'As a matter of fact, young sir,' Threepio went on, 'I'm not even sure which planet I'm on.'

The youth shook his head irritably. 'Never mind the "sir" – it's just Luke. And this world is called Tatooine.'

Threepio nodded. 'Thank you, Luke, s– Luke. I am See Threepio, human-droid relations specialist.' He jerked a metal thumb back towards the recharge unit. 'That is my companion, Artoo Detoo.'

'Pleased to meet you, Threepio,' Luke said easily. 'You too, Artoo.' Walking across the garage to the recharger, Luke bent over Artoo and began scraping at several bumps in the small 'droid's top with a chromed pick. Occasionally he jerked back sharply as bits of corrosion were flicked into the air by the tiny tool. 'There's a lot of strange carbon scoring here. Looks like you've both seen a lot of action out of the ordinary.'

'Indeed, sir,' Threepio admitted. 'Sometimes I'm amazed we're in as good shape as we are.' He added as an afterthought, 'What with the rebellion and all.'

A blaze appeared in Luke's eyes. 'You know about the rebellion against the Empire?' he demanded.

'In a way,' Threepio confessed. 'The rebellion was responsible for our coming into your service. We are refugees, you see.'

'*Refugees!* Then I *did* see a space battle!' He rambled on rapidly, excited. 'Tell me where you've been – in how many encounters. How is the rebellion going? Does the Empire take it seriously? Have you seen many ships destroyed?'

'A bit slower, please, sir,' Threepio pleaded. 'You misinterpret our status. We were innocent bystanders. Our involvement with the rebellion was of the most marginal nature.

'As to battles, we were in several, I think. It is difficult to tell when one is not directly in contact with the actual battle machinery.' He shrugged. 'Remember, sir, I am little more than a cosmeticised interpreter and not very good at telling stories or relating histories. I am a very literal machine.'

Luke turned away, disappointed, and returned to his cleaning of Artoo Detoo. Additional scraping turned up a small metal fragment tightly lodged between two bar conduits that would normally form a linkage. Setting down the delicate pick, Luke switched to a larger instrument.

'Well, my little friend,' he murmured, 'you've got something jammed in here real good.' As he pushed and pried Luke directed half his attention to Threepio. 'Were you on a star freighter or was it – '

Metal gave way with a powerful *crack*, and the recoil sent Luke tumbling head over heels. Getting to his feet, he started to curse – then froze.

The front of the Artoo unit had begun to glow, exuding a three-dimensional image less than one-third of a metre square but precisely defined.

Despite a superficial sharpness, the image flickered and jiggled unsteadily, as if the recording had been made and installed with haste. Luke stared at the foreign colours and started to form a question. But it was never finished. The lips on the figure moved, and the girl spoke – or rather, seemed to speak. Luke knew the aural accompaniment was generated somewhere within Artoo Detoo's squat torso.

'Obi-wan Kenobi,' the voice implored huskily, 'help me! You're my only remaining hope.' A burst of static dissolved the face momentarily. Then it coalesced again, and once more the voice repeated, 'Obi-wan Kenobi, you're my only remaining hope.'

Luke sat perfectly still for a moment, then he directed his words to the Artoo unit.

'What's this all about, Artoo Detoo?'

The stubby 'droid shifted slightly, the cubish portrait shifting with him, and beeped.

Threepio appeared as mystified as Luke. 'What is that?' he inquired sharply, gesturing at the speaking portrait and then at Luke. 'You were asked a question. What and who is that, and how are you originating it – and why?'

The Artoo unit generated a beep, followed by a whistling stream of information.

Threepio digested the data. 'He insists it's nothing, sir. Merely a malfunction – old data. A tape that should have been erased but was missed. He insists we pay it no mind.'

'Who is she?' he demanded, staring enraptured at the hologram. 'She's beautiful.'

38

'I really don't know who she is,' Threepio confessed. 'I think she might have been a passenger on our last voyage. From what I recall, she was a personage of some importance. This might have something to do with the fact that our Captain was attaché to – '

Luke cut him off. 'Is there any more to this recording? It sounds incomplete.' Getting to his feet, Luke reached out for the Artoo unit.

The robot moved backward and produced whistles of such frantic concern that Luke hesitated and held off reaching for the internal controls.

'It's all right – he's our master now.' Threepio indicated Luke. 'You can trust him.'

Detoo appeared to hesitate, uncertain. Then he whistled and beeped a long complexity at his friend.

'Well?' Luke prompted impatiently.

Threepio paused before replying. 'He says that he is the property of one Obi-wan Kenobi, a resident of this world. Of this very region, in fact. The sentence fragment we are hearing is part of a private message intended for this person.'

Threepio shook his head slowly. 'Quite frankly, sir, I don't know what he's talking about. Our last master was Captain Colton. I never heard Artoo mention a prior master. I've certainly never heard of an Obi-wan Kenobi.'

'Obi-wan Kenobi,' Luke recited thoughtfully. His expression suddenly brightened. 'Say . . . I wonder if he could be referring to old Ben Kenobi.'

'Begging your pardon,' Threepio gulped, 'but you actually know of such a person?'

'Not exactly,' he admitted. 'I don't know anyone named Obi-wan – but old Ben lives somewhere out on the fringe of the Western Dune Sea. He's kind of a local character – a hermit. Uncle Owen and a few of the other farmers say he's a sorcerer.

'He comes around once in a while to trade things. My uncle usually runs him off.' He paused and glanced at the small robot again. 'But I never heard that old Ben owned a 'droid of any kind.'

Luke's gaze was drawn irresistibly back to the hologram. 'I wonder who she is. She must be important – especially if what you told me just now is true, Threepio. She sounds and looks as if she's in some kind of trouble. Maybe the message *is* important. We ought to hear the rest of it.'

He reached again for the Artoo's internal controls, and the robot scurried backward again, squeaking a blue streak.

'He says there's a restraining separator bolt that's circuiting out his self-motivation components.' Threepio translated. 'He suggests that if you move the bolt he might be able to repeat the entire message,' Threepio finished uncertainly.

Luke shook himself.

'I see it, I think.'

Selecting the proper tool, Luke reached into the exposed circuitry and popped the restraining bolt free. The portrait disappeared.

Luke stood back. 'Where did she go?' he finally prompted. 'Make her come back. Play the entire message, Artoo Detoo.'

An innocent-sounding beep came from the robot. Threepio translated. 'He said, "What message?"'

Threepio's attention turned angrily to his companion. 'You know what message! The one you just played a fragment of for us.'

Artoo sat and hummed softly to himself.

'I'm sorry, sir,' Threepio said slowly, 'but he shows signs of having developed an alarming flutter in his obedience-rational module. Perhaps if we –'

A voice from down a corridor interrupted him . . . 'Luke – come to dinner!'

Luke rose and turned away from the puzzling little 'droid. 'Okay,' he called. 'I'm coming, Aunt Beru!' He lowered his voice as he spoke to Threepio. 'See what you can do with him. I'll be back soon.'

40

As soon as the human was gone, Threepio whirled on his shorter companion. 'You'd better consider playing that whole recording for him,' he growled, with a suggestive nod towards a workbench laden with dismembered machine parts. 'Otherwise he's liable to take up that cleaning pick again and go digging for it. He might not be too careful what he cuts through if he believes you're deliberately withholding something from him.'

FOUR

'I think that Artoo unit might have been stolen, Uncle Owen,' Luke was saying, as if that had been the topic of conversation all along.

His uncle helped himself to the milk pitcher, mumbling his reply around a mouthful of food. 'What makes you think that?'

'For one thing, it's in awfully good shape for a discard. It generated a hologram recording while I was cleaning – ' Luke tried to conceal his horror at the slip. He added hastily, 'But that's not important. The reason I think it might be stolen is because it claims to be the property of someone it calls Obi-wan Kenobi.'

Owen continued eating without looking up at his nephew. 'I thought,' Luke continued determinedly, 'it might be old Ben. The first name is different, but the last is identical.'

When his uncle steadfastly maintained his silence, Luke prompted him directly. 'Do *you* know who he's talking about, Uncle Owen?'

His uncle looked uncomfortable instead of angry. 'It's nothing,' he mumbled, still not meeting Luke's gaze. 'A name from another time that can only mean trouble.'

Luke refused to heed the implied warning and pressed

on. 'Is it someone related to old Ben, then? I didn't know he had any relatives.'

'You stay away from that old wizard, you hear me!' his uncle exploded, awkwardly substituting threat for reason. 'I've told you about Kenobi before. He's a crazy old man; he's dangerous and full of mischief.

'That 'droid has nothing to do with him. Couldn't have,' he grumbled half to himself. 'Recording – huh! Well, tomorrow I want you to take the unit into Anchorhead and have its memory flushed.'

Snorting, he bent to his half-eaten meal. 'That will be the end of this foolishness. I don't care where that machine thinks it came from. I paid hard credit for it, and it belongs to us now.'

'But suppose it *does* belong to someone else,' Luke wondered. 'What if this Obi-wan person comes looking for his 'droid?'

An expression between sorrow and a sneer crossed his uncle's face. 'He won't. I don't think that man exists any more. He died about the same time as your father. Now forget about it.'

'Then he *was* a real person,' Luke murmured. 'Did he know my father?'

'I said forget about it,' Owen snapped. 'Your only worry as far as those two 'droids are concerned is having them ready for work tomorrow.'

'You know,' Luke replied distantly, 'I think these 'droids are going to work out fine. In fact, I want to transmit my application to enter the Academy for next year.'

Owen scowled.

'You have more than enough 'droids now, and they're in good condition. They'll last.

'But 'droids can't replace a man, Luke,' his uncle said. 'You know that. The harvest is when I need you the most. It's just for one more season after this one.'

Luke toyed with his food, saying nothing.

'Listen,' his uncle told him, 'for the first time we've

got a chance for a real fortune. We'll make enough to hire some extra hands for next time. Not 'droids – people. Then you can go to the Academy.'

'It's another *year*,' his nephew objected sullenly.

Owen shrugged the objection off. 'Time will pass before you know it.'

Abruptly Luke rose, shoving his barely touched plate of food aside. 'That's what you said last year when Biggs left.' He spun and half ran from the room.

'Where are you going, Luke?' his aunt yelled worriedly after him.

Luke's reply was bleak, bitter. 'Looks like I'm going nowhere.'

Silence hung in the air of the dining-room after Luke departed. Husband and wife ate mechanically. Eventually Aunt Beru looked up, and pointed out earnestly, 'Owen, you can't keep him here forever. Most of his friends are gone. The Academy means so much to him.'

Listlessly her husband replied, 'I'll make it up to him next year. I promise. We'll have money – or maybe, the year after that.'

'Luke's just not a farmer, Owen,' she continued firmly. 'He never will be, no matter how hard you try to make him one.' She shook her head slowly. 'He's got too much of his father in him.'

For the first time all evening Owen Lars looked thoughtful as well as concerned. 'That's what I'm afraid of,' he whispered.

Luke had gone topside. He stood on the sand watching the double sunset as first one and then the other of Tatooine's twin suns sank slowly behind the distant range of dunes. In the fading light the sands turned gold, russet, and flaming red-orange before advancing night put the bright colours to sleep for another day.

As the night cold came creeping over the sand, he brushed the grit from his trousers and descended into the garage. Maybe working on the 'droids would bury some of the remorse a little. But a quick survey of the

43

chamber showed no movement. Neither of the new machines was in sight. Frowning slightly, Luke took a small control box from his belt and activated a couple of switches.

A low hum came from the box. The caller produced Threepio. Luke started towards him. 'What are you hiding back there for?'

The robot came stumbling around the prow of the craft. The Artoo unit was still nowhere to be seen.

The reason for his absence came pouring unbidden from Threepio. 'It wasn't my fault,' the robot begged frantically. 'Please don't deactivate me! I told him not to go, but he's faulty. He must be malfunctioning. He kept babbling on about some sort of mission, sir.'

'You mean . . . ?' Luke started to gape.

'Yes, sir . . . he's gone.'

'And I removed his restraining coupling myself,' Luke muttered slowly. Already he could visualize his uncle's face. The last of their savings was tied up in these 'droids.

Racing out of the garage, Luke hunted for reasons why the Artoo unit should go berserk. Threepio followed on his heels.

From a small ridge which formed the highest point close by the homestead, Luke had a panoramic view of the surrounding desert. Bringing out the macro-binoculars, he scanned the rapidly darkening horizons for something small, metallic, three-legged, and out of its mechanical mind.

The binoculars finally came down, and Luke commented, 'He's nowhere in sight.' He kicked furiously at the ground. 'Damn it – how could I have been so stupid, letting it trick me into removing that restrainer! Uncle Owen's going to kill me.'

'Begging your pardon, sir,' ventured a hopeful Threepio, 'but can't we go after him?'

Luke turned. He examined the wall of black advancing towards them. 'Not at night. It's too dangerous with all the raiders around. I'm not too concerned about the jawas, but sandpeople. We'll have to wait until morning to try to track him.'

A shout rose from the homestead below. 'Luke – Luke, are you finished with those 'droids yet? I'm turning down the power for the night.'

'All right!' Luke responded, sidestepping the question. 'I'll be down in a few minutes, Uncle Owen!' Turning, he took one last look at the vanished horizon. 'Boy, am I in for it!' he muttered. 'That little 'droid's going to get me in a lot of trouble.'

'Have you seen Luke this morning?' Owen asked Beru.

She glanced briefly at him, then returned to her cooking. 'Yes. He said he had some things to do before he started out to the south ridge this morning, so he left early.'

'Before breakfast?' Owen frowned. 'That's not like him. Did he take the new 'droids with him?'

'I think so. I'm sure I saw at least one of them with him.'

'Well,' Owen mused, 'he'd better have those ridge units repaired by midday or there'll be hell to pay.'

A face shielded by smooth white metal emerged from the half-buried life pod that now formed the backbone of a dune slightly higher than its neighbours. The voice sounded tired.

'Nothing,' the inspecting trooper muttered to his companions. 'No tapes, and no sign of habitation.'

Powerful handguns lowered at the information that the pod was deserted. One of the armoured men turned, calling to an officer standing some distance away. 'This is definitely the pod that cleared the rebel ship, sir, but there's nothing on board.'

'Yet it set down intact,' the officer murmured to himself. 'It *could* have done so on automatics, but they shouldn't have been engaged.' Something didn't make sense.

'Here's why there's nothing on board and no hint of life, sir,' a voice declared.

The officer strode to where another trooper was kneeling in the sand. He held up an object for the officer's inspection. It shone in the sun.

''Droid plating,' the officer observed after a quick glance at the metal fragment. Superior and underling exchanged a significant glance. Then their eyes turned simultaneously to the high mesas to the north.

Gravel and fine sand formed a gritty fog beneath the landspeeder as it slid across the rippling wasteland of Tatooine. Occasionally the craft would jog slightly as it encountered a dip or slight rise, to return to its smooth passage as its pilot compensated for the change in terrain.

Luke leaned back in the seat, as Threepio skilfully directed the landcraft around dunes and rocky outcrops. 'You handle a landspeeder pretty well, for a machine,' he noted admiringly.

'Thank you, sir,' Threepio responded, his eyes never moving from the landscape ahead. 'Versatility is my middle name. I have been called upon to perform unexpected functions which would have appalled my designers.'

'Old Ben Kenobi is supposed to live out in this general direction. Even though nobody knows exactly where. I don't see how that Artoo unit could have come this far so quickly.' His expression was downcast. 'We must have missed him back in the dunes somewhere. He could be anywhere out here. And Uncle Owen must be wondering why I haven't called in from the south ridge.'

But something more important than his uncle was on Luke's mind at the moment. 'Wait a minute,' he advised Threepio as he stared at the instrument panel. 'There's something dead ahead on the metal scanner. Can't distinguish outlines at this distance, but judging by size, it *could* be our wandering 'droid. Hit it.'

The landspeeder jumped forward as Threepio engaged the accelerator, but its occupants were totally unaware that other eyes were watching as the craft increased its speed.

Those eyes were not organic, but they weren't wholly mechanical, either. No one could say for certain, because no one had ever made that intimate a study of the Tusken Raiders – known to the margin farmers of Tatooine simply as the sandpeople.

The Tuskens didn't permit close study of themselves, discouraging potential observers by methods as effective as they were uncivilised. A few thought they must be related to the jawas.

Both races affected tight clothing to shield them from Tatooine's twin solar radiation, but there comparisons ended. Instead of heavy woven cloaks like the jawas wore, the sandpeole wrapped themselves mummy-like in endless swathings and bandages and loose bits of cloth.

Where the jawas feared everything, a Tusken Raider feared little. The sandpeople were larger, stronger, and far more aggressive. Fortunately for the human colonists of Tatooine, they were not very numerous and elected to pursue their nomadic existence in some of Tatooine's most desolate regions. Contact between human and Tusken, therefore, was infrequent and uneasy.

One of the pair felt that that unstable condition had temporarily shifted in his favour, and he was about to take full advantage of it as he raised his rifle towards the landspeeder. But his companion grabbed the weapon and shoved down on it before it could be fired. This set off a violent argument between the two. And, as they traded vociferous opinions, the landspeeder sped on its way.

The two broke off the discussion and scrambled down the back side of the high ridge. Two Banthas stirred at the approach of their masters. Each was as large as a small dinosaur, with bright eyes and long, thick fur.

They hissed anxiously as the sandpeople approached, then mounted them from knee to saddle.

With a kick the Banthas rose. Moving slowly but with enormous strides, the two massive horned creatures swept down the back of the rugged bluff, urged on by their anxious mahouts.

'It's him, all right,' Luke declared with mixed anger and satisfaction as the tiny tripodal form came into view. The speeder banked and swung down on to the floor of a huge sandstone canyon. Luke slipped his rifle out from behind the seat and swung it over his shoulder. 'Come round in front of him, Threepio,' he instructed.

The Artoo unit obviously noted their approach, but made no move to escape; it simply halted as soon as it detected them and waited until the craft swung around in a smooth arc and came to a sharp halt.

After finishing a cautious survey of the canyon, Luke led his companion out on to the gravelly surface and up to Artoo Detoo. 'Just where,' he inquired sharply, 'did you think you were going?'

A feeble whistle issued from the apologetic robot, but it was Threepio and not the recalcitrant rover who was doing most of the talking.

'Master Luke here is now your rightful owner, Artoo. Now that he's found you, let's have no more of this "Obi-wan Kenobi" gibberish.'

Artoo started to beep in protest, but Threepio's indignation was too great to permit excuses. 'And don't talk to me about your mission. You're fortunate Master Luke doesn't blast you into a million pieces right here and now.'

'Not much chance of that,' admitted Luke. He eyed the rapidly rising suns. 'I just hope we can get back before Uncle Owen really lets go.'

'If you don't mind my saying so,' Threepio suggested, 'I think you ought to deactivate the little fugitive until you've gotten him safely back in the garage.'

'No. He's not going to try anything.' Luke studied the

48

softly beeping 'droid sternly. 'I hope he's learned his lesson. There's no need to –'

Without warning the Artoo unit suddenly leaped off the ground – no mean feat considering the weakness of the spring mechanisms in his three thick legs. His cylindrical body was twisting and spinning as he let out a frantic symphony of whistles, hoots, and electronic exclamations.

Luke was not alarmed. 'What is it? What's wrong with him now?' He was beginning to see how Threepio's patience could be worn thin. He had had enough of this addled instrument himself.

'Oh my, sir. Artoo claims there are several creatures of unknown type approaching from the south-east.'

That *could* be another attempt by Artoo to distract them, but Luke couldn't take the chance. Instantly he had his rifle off his shoulder and had activated the energy cell. He examined the horizon and saw nothing. But then, sandpeople were experts at making themselves unseeable.

Luke suddenly realised exactly how far out they were, how much ground the landspeeder had covered that morning. 'Let's take a look,' he decided.

Moving cautiously forward and keeping his rifle ready, he led Threepio towards the crest of a nearby high dune. At the same time he took care not to let Artoo out of his sight.

Once at the top he lay flat and traded his rifle for the macrobinoculars. Below, another canyon spread out before them, rising to a wind-weathered wall of rust and ochre. Advancing the binocs slowly across the canyon floor, he settled unexpectedly on two tethered shapes. Banthas – and riderless!

'Did you say something, sir?' wheezed Threepio, struggling up behind Luke. His locomotors were not designed for such outer climbing and scrambling.

'Banthas, all right,' Luke whispered over his shoulder.

He looked back into the eyepieces, refocusing slightly. 'Wait . . . it's sandpeople. I see one of them.'

Something dark suddenly blocked his sight. For a moment he thought that a rock might have moved in front of him. Irritably he dropped the binoculars and reached out to move the blinding object aside. His hand touched something like soft metal.

It was a bandaged leg as big around as both of Luke's together. Shocked, he looked up . . . and up. The towering figure glaring down at him was no jawa. It had seemingly erupted straight from the sand.

Threepio took a startled step backward and found no footing. As gyros whined in protest the tall robot tumbled backward down the side of the dune. Frozen in place, Luke heard steadily fading bangs and rattles as Threepio bounced down the steep slope behind him.

The Tusken let out a terrifying grunt of fury and pleasure and brought down his heavy gaderffii. Luke threw the rifle up in a gesture more instinctive than calculated. Made from cannibalised freighter plating, the huge axe shattered the barrel and made metallic confetti of the gun's delicate insides.

Luke scrambled backward and found himself against a steep drop. The Raider stalked him slowly, weapon held high over its rag-enclosed head. It uttered a gruesome, chuckling laugh.

Luke tried to view his situation objectively, as he had been instructed to do in survival school. Trouble was, his mouth was dry, his hands were shaking, and he was paralysed with fear. With the Raider in front of him and a probably fatal drop behind, something else in his mind took over and opted for the least painful response. He fainted.

None of the Raiders noticed Artoo Detoo as the tiny robot forced himself into a small alcove in the rocks near the landspeeder. One of them was carrying the inert form of Luke. He dumped the unconscious youth in a heap next to the speeder, then joined his fellows as they began swarming over the open craft.

Supplies and spare parts were thrown in all directions. From time to time the plundering would be interrupted as several of them quibbled or fought over a choice bit of booty.

Unexpectedly, distribution of the landspeeder's contents ceased, and with frightening speed the Raiders became part of the desertscape.

Far off to the west, something howled. A rolling, booming drone ricocheted off canyon walls.

The sandpeople remained poised a moment longer. Then they were uttering loud grunts and moans of fright as they rushed to get away.

The shivering howl sounded again, nearer this time. By now the sandpeople were half-way to their waiting Banthas, that were lowing tensely and tugging at their tethers.

Although the sound held no meaning for Artoo Detoo, the little 'droid tried to squeeze himself even deeper into the almost-cave.

Not even the dust of their passing remained to mark where the Tusken Raiders had been dismembering the interior of the landspeeder. Artoo Detoo shut down all but vital functions, trying to minimise noise and light as a swishing sound grew gradually audible. Moving towards the landspeeder, the creature appeared above the top of a nearby dune ...

FIVE

It was tall, but hardly monstrous, looking very much like an old man. He was clad in a shabby cloak and loose robes hung with a few small straps, packs, and unrecognisable instruments. It was impossible to tell where his attire ended and his skin began. That aged visage blended into the cloth, and his beard appeared but an extension of the loose threads covering his upper chest.

A questing beak of nose, like a high rock, protruded outward from a flashflood of wrinkles and scars. The eyes bordering it were a liquid crystal-azure. The man smiled through sand and dust and beard, squinting at the crumpled form lying alongside the landspeeder.

Artoo shifted his position slightly, trying to obtain a better view. The sound produced by a tiny pebble he dislodged was barely perceptible to his electronic sensors, but the man whirled as if shot. He stared straight at Artoo's alcove, still smiling gently.

'Hello there,' he called. 'Come here, my little friend. No need to be afraid.'

Waddling out into the sunlight, Artoo made his way over to where Luke lay.

The old man bent beside Luke and reached out to touch his forehead, then his temple. Shortly, the unconscious youth was stirring and mumbling like a dreaming sleeper.

'Don't worry,' the human told Artoo, 'he'll be all right.'

Luke blinked, stared upward, and muttered, 'What happened?'

'Rest easy, son,' the man instructed him as he sat back on his heels. 'You've had a busy day.' Again the boyish grin. 'You're mighty lucky your head's still attached to the rest of you.'

'Ben . . . it's got to be!' A sudden remembrance made Luke look around fearfully. But there was no sign of sandpeople. Slowly he raised his body to a sitting position. 'Ben Kenobi . . . am I glad to see you!'

Rising, the old man surveyed the canyon floor and rolling rimwall above. 'The Jundland wastes are not to be travelled lightly. It's the misguided traveller who tempts the Tuskens' hospitality.' His gaze went back to his patient. 'Tell me, young man, what brings you this far into nowhere?'

Luke indicated Artoo Detoo. 'This little 'droid. For a while I thought he'd gone crazy, claiming he was searching for a former master. Now I don't think so. I've never seen such devotion in a 'droid – misguided or otherwise. There seems to be no stopping him; he even resorted to tricking me.'

Luke's gaze shifted upward. 'He claims to be the property of someone called Obi-wan Kenobi. Is that a relative of yours?'

Kenobi appeared to ponder the question. 'Obi-wan Kenobi!' he recited. 'Obi-wan . . . now, that's a name I haven't heard in a long time. A long time. Most curious.'

Luke climbed excitedly to his feet, all thoughts of Tusken Raiders forgotten. 'You know him, then?'

A smile split that collage of wrinkled skin and beard. 'Of course I know him: he's me. But I haven't gone by the name *Obi-wan*, though, since before you were born.'

'Then,' Luke essayed, gesturing at Artoo Detoo, 'this 'droid does belong to you, as he claims.'

'Now, that's the peculiar part,' Kenobi confessed. 'I can't seem to remember owning a 'droid, least of all a modern Artoo unit. Most interesting.'

Something drew the old man's gaze to the brow of nearby cliffs. 'I think it's best we make use of your land-speeder. The sandpeople are easily startled, but they'll soon return in greater numbers.'

'I won't argue that.' Luke was rubbing at the back of his head. 'Let's get started.'

That was when Artoo let out a pathetic beep and whirled. Luke suddenly comprehended the reason behind it. 'Threepio.' Luke exclaimed, worriedly. Artoo was already moving as fast as possible away from the landspeeder. 'Come on, Ben.'

The little robot led them to the edge of a large sand-pit. It stopped there, pointing downward and squeaking mournfully.

Threepio lay in the sand at the base of the slope down which he had tumbled. His casing was dented and badly mangled. One arm lay broken and bent a short distance away.

'*Threepio!*' Luke called. There was no response. Opening a plate on the robot's back, Luke flipped a hidden switch on and off several times in succession.

Using his remaining arm, Threepio rolled over and sat up. 'Where am I,' he murmured.

'You're lucky any of your main circuits are still operational,' Luke informed him. He looked significantly toward the top of the hill. 'We've got to get out of here before the sandpeople return.'

With Luke and Ben Kenobi's aid, the battered 'droid somehow managed to struggle erect. Little Artoo watched from the pit's rim.

Hesitating part way up the slope, Kenobi sniffed the air suspiciously. 'Quickly, son. They're on the move again.'

Trying to watch the surrounding rocks and his footsteps simultaneously, Luke fought to drag Threepio clear of the pit.

The decor of Ben Kenobi's well-concealed cave was Spartan without appearing uncomfortable. The living area radiated an aura of lean comfort with more importance attached to metal comforts than those of the awkward human body.

Luke spent several hours in the corner which was equipped as a compact yet complete repair shop, working to fix Threepio's severed arm.

While Luke was thus occupied, Kenobi's attention was concentrated on Artoo Detoo. The squat 'droid sat passively on the cool cavern floor while the old man fiddled with its metal insides. Finally the man sat back and closed the open panels in the robot's rounded head. 'Now let's see if we can figure out what you are, my little friend, and where you came from.'

Luke was almost finished, and Kenobi's words were sufficient to pull him away from the repair area. 'I saw part of the message,' he began, 'and I . . . '

Once more the striking portrait was being projected into empty space from the front of the little robot. Luke broke off, enraptured by its enigmatic beauty once again.

'Yes, I think that's got it,' Kenobi murmured.

The image continued to flicker, indicating a tape hastily prepared. But it was much sharper, better defined now. Kenobi was skilled in more subjects than desert scavenging.

'General Obi-wan Kenobi,' the mellifluous voice was saying, 'I present myself in the name of the world family of Alderaan and of the Alliance to Restore the Republic. I break your solitude at the bidding of my father, Bail Organa, Viceroy and First Chairman of the Alderaan system.'

Kenobi absorbed this extraordinary declamation while Luke's eyes bugged big enough to fall from his face.

'Years ago, General,' the voice continued, 'you served the Old Republic in the Clone Wars. Now my father begs you to aid us again in our most desperate hour. He would have you join him on Alderaan. You *must* go to him.

'I regret that I am unable to present my father's request to you in person. My mission to meet with you has failed. Hence I have been forced to resort to this secondary method of communication.

'Information vital to the survival of the Alliance has been secured in the mind of this Detoo 'droid. My father will know how to retrieve it. I plead with you to see this unit safely delivered to Alderaan.'

She paused, and when she continued, her words were hurried and less laced with formality. 'You *must* help me, Obi-wan Kenobi. You are my last hope. I will be captured by agents of the Empire. They will learn nothing from me. Everything to be learned lies locked in the memory cells of this 'droid. Do not fail us, Obi-wan Kenobi. Do not fail *me*.'

A small cloud of tridimensional static replaced the delicate portrait, then it vanished entirely. Artoo Detoo gazed up expectantly at Kenobi.

If the breathless, anxiety message the unknown woman had just spoken had affected Kenobi in any way he gave no hint of it. Instead, he leaned back against the rock wall and tugged thoughtfully at his beard, puffing slowly on a water pipe.

Luke visualised that simple yet lovely portrait. 'She's so – so – ' Suddenly something in the message caused him to stare disbelievingly at the oldster. 'General Kenobi, you fought in the Clone Wars? But . . . that was so long ago.'

'Um, yes,' Kenobi acknowledged, 'I guess it was a while back. I was a Jedi knight once. Like,' he added, watching the youth appraisingly, 'your father.'

'A Jedi knight,' Luke echoed. Then he looked confused. 'But my father didn't fight in the Clone Wars. He was no knight – just a navigator on a space freighter.'

Kenobi's smile enfolded the pipe's mouthpiece. 'Or so your uncle has told you. Owen Lars didn't agree with your father's ideas, opinions, or with his philosophy of life. He believed that your father should have stayed here on Tatooine and not gotten involved in . . . ' Again the seemingly indifferent shrug.

Luke said nothing, his body tense as the old man related bits and pieces of a personal history Luke had viewed only through his uncle's distortions.

'Owen was always afraid that your father's adventurous life might influence you, might pull you away from Anchorhead. I'm afraid there wasn't much of the farmer in your father.'

Luke turned away. 'I wish I'd known him,' he finally whispered.

'He was the best pilot I ever knew,' Kenobi went on, 'and a smart fighter. The force . . . the instinct was strong in him. He was also a good friend.'

Suddenly the boyish twinkle returned to those piercing eyes. 'I understand you're quite a pilot yourself.'

Kenobi's look of evaluation made Luke nervous. 'You've grown up quite a bit since the last time I saw you.'

Luke waited silently as Kenobi sank back into deep contemplation. After a while the old man stirred. 'All this reminds me,' he declared with deceptive casualness. 'I have something here for you.' He walked over to a bulky, old-fashioned chest and started rummaging through it.

'When you were old enough,' Kenobi was saying, 'your father wanted you to have this . . . if I can find the blasted device. I tried to give it to you once before, but your uncle wouldn't allow it. He believed you might get some crazy ideas from it and follow old Obi-wan on some idealistic crusade.'

Kenobi handed Luke a small, innocuous-looking device, which the youth studied with interest.

It consisted of a short, thick handgrip with a couple of small switches set into the grip. Above this small post was a circular metal disc barely larger in diameter than his spread palm. A number of unfamiliar, jewel-like components were built into both handle and disc, including what looked like the smallest power cell Luke had ever seen. The reverse side of the disc was polished to mirror brightness. But it was the power cell that puzzled Luke the most. Whatever the thing was, it required a great deal of energy, according to the rating form of the cell.

Despite the claim that it had belonged to his father, the gizmo looked newly manufactured. Kenobi had obviously kept it carefully. Only a number of minute scratches on the handgrip hinted at previous usage.

'Your father's lightsabre,' Kenobi told him. 'At one time they were widely used. Still are, in certain galactic quarters.'

Luke examined the controls on the handle, then tentatively touched a brightly coloured button up near the mirrored pommel. Instantly the disc put forth a blue-white beam as thick as his thumb. It was dense to the point of opacity and a little over a metre in length. It did not fade, but remained brilliant and intense. Strangely, Luke felt no heat from it, though he was very careful not to touch it. He knew a lightsabre could drill a hole right through the rock wall of Kenobi's cave – or through a human being.

'This was the formal weapon of a Jedi knight,' explained Kenobi. 'Not as clumsy or random as a blaster. To use a lightsabre *well* was a mark of someone a cut above the ordinary.' He was pacing the floor of the cave as he spoke. .

'For over a thousand generations, Luke, the Jedi knights were the most powerful, most respected force in the galaxy. They served as the guardians and guarantors of peace and justice in the Old Republic.'

'How,' Luke asked slowly, 'did my father die?'

Kenobi hesitated. Unlike Owen Lars, he was unable to take refuge in a comfortable lie.

'He was betrayed and murdered,' Kenobi declared solemnly, 'by a young Jedi named Darth Vader. A boy I was training. One of my brightest disciples . . . one of my greatest failures.'

Kenobi resumed his pacing. 'Vader used the training I gave him and the force within him for evil, to help the later corrupt Emperors. With the Jedi knights disbanded, disorganised, or dead, there were few to oppose Vader. Today they are all but extinct.'

An indecipherable expression crossed Kenobi's face. 'I wish I knew what Vader was after. I have the feeling he is marking time in preparation for some incomprehensible abomination. Such is the destiny of one who masters the force and is consumed by its dark side.'

Luke's face twisted in confusion. 'A force? That's the second time you've mentioned a "force".'

Kenobi nodded. 'Let us say simply that the force is something a Jedi must deal with. It has never been properly explained. Scientists have theorised it is an energy field generated by living things. Early man suspected its existence, yet remained in ignorance of its potential for millennia.

'Only certain individuals could recognise the force for what it was. They were mercilessly labelled: charlatans, fakers, mystics – and worse. Even fewer could make use of it. As it was usually beyond their primitive controls, it frequently was too powerful for them. They were misunderstood by their fellows – and worse.'

Kenobi made a wide, all-encompassing gesture with both arms. 'The force surrounds each and every one of us. Some men believe it directs our actions, and not the other way around. Knowledge of the force and how to manipulate it was what gave the Jedi his special power.'

Kenobi stared at Luke. When he spoke again it was in a tone so crisp that Luke jumped. 'You must learn the ways of the force, Luke – if you are to come with me to Alderaan.'

Luke hopped off the repair seat, looking dazed. 'I'm not going to Alderaan. I don't even know where Alderaan is.' He looked around wildly, trying to avoid the piercing gaze of Ben Kenobi . . . old Ben . . . crazy Ben . . .General Obi-wan . . .

'I've got to get back home,' he found himself muttering. 'It's late. I'm in for it as it is.' He gestured towards the motionless bulk of Artoo Detoo. 'You can keep the 'droid. He seems to want you to. I'll think of something to tell my uncle – I hope,' he added forlornly.

'I need your help, Luke,' Kenobi explained. 'I'm getting too old for this kind of thing. Can't trust myself to finish it properly on my own. This mission is far too important.' He nodded towards Artoo Detoo. 'You heard and saw the message.'

'But . . . I can't get involved with anything like that,' protested Luke. 'I've got work to do; we've got crops to bring in.'

'That sounds like your uncle talking,' Kenobi observed without rancour.

'Oh! My Uncle Owen . . . How am I going to explain all this to him?'

The old man suppressed a smile, aware that Luke's destiny had already been determined for him.

'Remember, Luke, the suffering of one man is the suffering of all. If not stopped soon enough, evil eventually reaches out to engulf all men.'

'I suppose,' Luke confessed nervously, 'I *could* take

you as far as Anchorhead. You can get transport from there to Mos Eisley, or wherever it is you want to go.'

'Very well,' agreed Kenobi. 'That will do for a beginning. Then you must do what you feel is *right*.'

The holding hole was deathly dim, with only the minimum of illumination provided, barely enough to see the black metal walls and the high ceiling overhead. The cell was designed to maximise a prisoner's feeling of helplessness. The single occupant started tensely as a hum came from one end of the chamber. The metal door began moving aside.

Straining to see outside, the girl saw several Imperial guards. Eyeing them defiantly, Leia Organa backed up against the far wall.

A monstrous black form entered the room, gliding smoothly as if on treads. Vader's presence crushed her spirit thoroughly. That villain was followed by an antiquated whip of a man, only slightly less terrifying, despite his miniscule appearance alongside the Dark Lord.

Darth Vader made a gesture to someone outside. Something that hummed like a huge bee slipped inside the doorway. Leia choked at the sight of the dark metal globe. It hung suspended on independent repulsors, a farrago of metal arms protruding from its sides. The arms were tipped with a multitude of delicate instruments.

Leia had heard rumours of such machines, but had never believed that Imperial technicians would construct such a monstrosity. Incorporated into its soulless memory was every barbarity, every outrage known to mankind.

Vader and Tarkin stood there quietly, giving her plenty of time to study the hovering nightmare. The Governor did not delude himself into thinking that mere presence of the device would shock her into giving up the information he needed. Not, he reflected, that the ensuing session would be especially unpleasant.

There was always enlightenment and knowledge to be gained from such encounters, and the Senator promised to be a most interesting subject.

He motioned to the machine. 'Now, Senator Organa, Princess Organa, we will discuss the location of the principal rebel base.'

The machine moved slowly towards her, travelling on a rising hum. Its indifferent spherical form blocked out Vader, the Governor, the rest of the cell . . . the light . . .

Muffled sounds penetrated the cell walls and thick door, drifting out into the hallway beyond. They barely intruded on the peace and quiet of the walkway running past the sealed chamber. Even so, the guards stationed immediately outside managed to edge a sufficient distance away to where those oddly modulated sounds could no longer be heard.

SIX

Topping a slight rise, the speeder dropped down a gentle slope into a broad, shallow canyon that was filled with twisted, burned shapes. Dead in the centre of this carnage lay the shattered hulk of a jawa sandcrawler.

Luke brought the speeder to a halt. Kenobi followed him on to the sand, and together they began to examine the detritus of destruction.

Several slight depressions in the sand caught Luke's attention. Walking a little faster, he came up next to them and studied them for a moment before calling back to Kenobi.

'Looks like the sandpeople did it, all right. Here's Bantha tracks . . . ' Luke shook his head in confusion. 'But I never heard of the Raiders hitting something this big.' He leaned back, staring up at the burned-out bulk of the sandcrawler.

Kenobi had passed him. He was examining the broad, huge footprints in the sand. 'They didn't,' he declared casually, 'but they intended that we should think so.'

Luke moved up alongside him. 'I don't understand, sir.'

'Look at these tracks carefully,' the older man directed him, pointing down at the nearest and then at the others. 'Whoever left here was riding Banthas side by side. Sandpeople always ride, single file, to hide their strength from any distant observers.'

Kenobi turned his attention to the sandcrawler. 'Look at the precision with which this firepower was applied. Sandpeople aren't this accurate. In fact, no one on Tatooine fires and destroys with this kind of efficiency.' Turning, he examined the horizon. One of those nearby bluffs concealed a secret – and a threat. 'Only Imperial troops would mount an attack with this kind of cold accuracy.'

Luke had walked over to one of the small, crumpled bodies and kicked it over on to its back.

'These are the same jawas who sold Uncle Owen and me Artoo and Threepio. Why would Imperial troops be slaughtering jawas and sandpeople? They must have killed some Raiders to get those Banthas.' He found himself growing unnaturally tense. 'But . . . if they tracked the 'droids to the jawas, then they had to learn who they sold them to. That would lead them back to . . .' Luke was sprinting insanely for the landspeeder.

'Luke, wait . . . wait, Luke!' Kenobi called. 'It's too dangerous! You'd never . . . !'

Luke heard nothing except the roaring in his ears, felt nothing save the burning in his heart. He jumped into the speeder. In an explosion of sand and gravel he left Kenobi and the two robots standing alone in the midst of smouldering bodies, framed by the smoking wreck of the sandcrawler.

He barely remembered to shut down the landspeeder's engine as he popped the cockpit canopy and threw himself out. Dark smoke was drifting steadily from holes in the ground.

Those holes had been his home. They might as well have been throats of small volcanoes now. Again and again he tried to penetrate the surface entrances to the below-ground complex, but the still-intense heat drove him back, coughing and choking.

Weakly he found himself stumbling clear. Half blinded, he staggered over to the exterior entrance to the garage. It too was burning. But perhaps they managed to escape in the other landspeeder.

'Aunt Beru . . . Uncle Owen!' Two smoking shapes showed down the tunnel, barely visible through tears and haze. They almost looked like – He squinted harder, wiping angrily at his uncooperative eyes.

No.

Then he was spinning away, falling to his stomach and burying his face in the sand so he wouldn't have to look any more.

The tridimensional solid screen filled one wall of the vast chamber from floor to ceiling. It showed a million star systems. A tiny portion of the galaxy.

Far below, the huge shape of Darth Vader stood flanked on one side by Governor Tarkin and on the other by Admiral Motti and General Tagge.

'The final checkout is complete.' Motti informed them. 'All systems are operational.' He turned to the others. 'What shall be the first course we set?'

Vader mumbled softly, half to himself, 'She has a surprising amount of control. Her resistance to the interrogator is considerable.' He glanced down at Tarkin. 'It will be some time before we can extract any useful information from her.'

'I've always found the methods you recommend rather quaint, Vader.'

'They are efficient,' the Dark Lord argued softly. 'In the interests of accelerating the procedure, however, I am open to your suggestions.'

Tarkin looked thoughtful. 'Such stubbornness can often be devoured by applying threats to something other than the one involved.'

'What do you mean?'

'I think it is time we demonstrated the full power of this station. We may do so in a fashion doubly useful.' He instructed Motti, 'Tell your programmers to set course for the Alderaan system.'

Working together, the two 'droids helped Kenobi throw the last of the bodies on to the blazing pyre, then stood back and watched the dead continue to burn. The desert scavengers would have been equally efficient in picking the burned-out sandcrawler clean of flesh, but Kenobi retained values most modern men would have deemed archaic. He would consign no one to the bonegnawers and gravel-maggots, not even a filthy jawa.

At a rising thrumming, Kenobi turned to see the landspeeder approaching. It slowed and hovered nearby, but showed no signs of life.

He started towards the waiting craft. The canopy flipped open to reveal Luke, motionless in the pilot's seat. He didn't look up at Kenobi's inquiring glance. That in itself was enough to tell the old man what had happened.

'I share your sorrow, Luke,' he ventured softly. 'There was nothing you could have done. Had you been there, you'd be dead now, too, and the 'droids would be in the hands of the Imperials. Not even the force – '

'Damn your force!' Luke snarled with sudden violence. There was a set to his jaw that belonged on a much older face.

'I'll take you to the spaceport at Mos Eisley, Ben. I want to go with you – to Alderaan. There's nothing left for me here now.' His eyes turned to look out across the desert, to focus on something beyond sand and rock and canyon walls. 'I want to learn to be like a Jedi, like my father. I want . . . '

Kenibo slid into the cockpit, put a hand gently on

Six years ago, George Lucas, the man who brought you AMERICAN GRAFFITI, began his first draft of a film that very well may become a milestone in the space fantasy genre.

The high-energy adventure unites the hardware of contemporary science fiction with the romantic fantasies of sword and sorcery.

STAR WARS is an imaginative entertainment experience which takes the audience to an unknown galaxy thousands of light years from earth.

Written and designed for the large screen, the live-action fantasy adventure film follows a young man, Luke Skywalker, through exotic worlds uniquely different from our own.

Beginning on the small arid planet of Tatooine, Luke plunges into an extraordinary intergalactic search for a kidnapped rebel Princess. His odyssey finally culminates in a wild, terrifying space battle over a large satellite battle station, Death Star.

Luke is joined by several friends—space pilots, outlaws, mechanical robots, and a large furry Wookie—and together they battle numerous villains and creatures in a massive Galactic Civil War.

Producer Gary Kurtz and writer-director George Lucas, the team responsible for the highly successful AMERICAN GRAFFITI, began production three years ago to create this impressive space adventure.

A whole new special effects shop was constructed to take advantage of computer technology to implement some of the most elaborate miniature and optical effects ever produced on film.

The same care has gone into casting the unusual roles. Lucas, casting with the same approach he used for AMERICAN GRAFFITI, chose new, fresh talent for three of the five major roles. In the other two roles, he cast British veterans, Alec Guinness and Peter Cushing.

"I think that anyone who goes to the movies loves to have an emotional experience. It's basic---whether you're seven, seventeen or seventy. The more intense the experience, the more successful the film.

"I've always loved adventure films. After I finished AMERICAN GRAFFITI, I came to realize that since the demise of the western, there hasn't been much in the mythological fantasy genre available to the film audience. So, instead of making "isn't-it-terrible-what's-happening-to-mankind" movies, which is how I began, I decided that I'd try to fill that gap. I'd make a film so rooted in imagination that the grimness of everyday life would not follow the audience into the theater. In other words, for two hours, they could forget.

"I'm trying to reconstruct a genre that's been lost and bring it to a new dimension so that the elements of space, fantasy, adventure, suspense and fun all work and feed off each other. So, in a way, STAR WARS is a movie for the kid in all of us."

— George Lucas

Luke Skywalker
• Mark Hamill

Ben (Obi-Wan) Kenobi
• Alec Guinness

Princess Leia Organa
• Carrie Fisher

Luke Skywalker, a twenty-year-old farmboy on the remote planet of Tatooine, is compelled to break from his dull chores on his Uncle's moisture farm. The cryptic message of a kidnapped Princess catapults the brave, impetuous hero into a series of adventures on various worlds of a distant galaxy. Accompanied by his two servant robots, Luke challenges the Galactic Empire's ultimate weapon, the Death Star.

Ben Kenobi, a once respected name in the galaxy, is now an outlaw in the Tatooine mountains. The shabby old desert-rat of a man was, before the rise of the sinister Galactic Empire, one of the greatest warriors in the Old Republic. Even now, in his old age he can still be a threat to the sovereignty of the Empire because of his very special powers.

Princess Leia the very young Senator from Alderaan, has been using her political position to secretly gather information against the Empire. The strong-willed, intelligent Princess has been a unifying force in bringing about the rebellion against the oppression of the powerful Galactic Empire.

Darth Vader

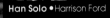

Han Solo • Harrison Ford

Grand Moff Tarkin
• Peter Cushing

Han Solo is the overly confident captain of the Millennium Falcon, a Corellian pirate starship. Accompanied by his Wookie companion, Chewbacca, he plies his mercenary trade outside the restrictive laws of the Empire. At times his insanely reckless manner pushes him into situations from which only his foolhardy courage can save him.

Darth Vader personifies the evil of the Galactic Empire. The awesome, malevolent figure dressed in flowing black robes keeps his face forever masked by a grotesque breath screen. He employs his extrasensory powers to keep the Emperor enthroned and to aid Governor Tarkin in the destruction of the rebellion.

Grand Moff Tarkin is the Governor of the Imperial Outland regions. His insatiable political ambitions to become Emperor have driven him to use ruthless means to quell the rapidly growing rebellion. To this end he has constructed a large and frighteningly powerful new battle station, the Death Star, which is capable of destroying an entire planet.

See-Threepio • C-3PO   **Artoo-Detoo •** R2-D2   **Chewbacca**

See-Threepio is a tall robot with a gleaming metallic surface. As a human-robot relations specialist he translates thousands of the Galactic languages, including the electronic tongues spoken by many robots. His human-like appearance is often matched with his human-like behavior as well.

Artoo-Detoo is a meter-high, cylindrical robot whose face is a mass of computer lights surrounding a single radar eye. Artoo, a sophisticated computer repair and information retrieval robot, can only speak to another robot in a series of electronic sounds. His thick clawed legs carry the feisty, rebellious automaton into a series of dangerous encounters.

Chewbacca, the hundred-year-old giant Wookie, co-pilots the Millennium Falcon. The huge anthropoid has a quasi-monkey face with large blue eyes that soften his awesome appearance. His language includes little more than a series of grunts which can reach a deafening crescendo when his temper is aroused.

the youth's shoulder, then went forward to make room for the two robots. 'I'll do my best to see that you get what you want, Luke. For now, let's go to Mos Eisley.'

Luke nodded and closed the canopy. The landspeeder moved away to the southeast, leaving behind the still-smouldering sandcrawler, the jawa funeral pyre, and the only life Luke had ever known.

'There it is,' Kenobi murmured, indicating the unimpressive collection of buildings, 'Mos Eisley Spaceport – the ideal place for us to lose ourselves while we seek passage offplanet. Not a more wretched collection of villainy and disreputable types exists anywhere on Tatooine. The Empire has been altered to us, so we must be very cautious, Luke. The population of Mos Eisley should disguise us well.'

Luke wore a determined look. 'I'm ready for anything, Obi-wan.'

Luke was manoeuvring the landspeeder through the town's outskirts when several tall, gleaming forms appeared and began to close a circle around him. For one panicked moment he considered gunning the engine and racing through the pedestrians and other vehicles. A firm grip on his arm restrained and relaxed him. He glanced over to see Kenobi smiling, warning him.

One of the troopers raised an armoured hand. Luke had no choice but to respond. As he pulled the speeder over, he grew aware of the attention they were receiving from curious passersby. It seemed that the trooper's attention was reserved for the two unmoving robots seated in the speeder behind them.

'How long have you had these 'droids?' the trooper who had raised his hand barked.

Looking blank for a second, Luke finally came up with 'Three or four seasons, I guess.'

'They're up for sale, if you want them – and the price is right,' Kenobi put in, giving a wonderful impression of a desert finagler out to cajole a few quick credits.

The trooper in charge did not reply. He was absorbed

in a thorough examination of the landspeeder's underside.

'Did you come in from the south?' he asked.

'No . . . no,' Luke answered quickly, 'we live in the west, near Bestine township.'

'Bestine?' the trooper murmured, walking around to study the speeder's front. He moved to stand ominously close to Luke and snapped, 'Let me see your identification.'

Kenobi leaned over and was talking easily to the trooper. 'You don't need to see his identification,' the old man informed the Imperial in a peculiar voice.

Staring blankly back at him, the officer replied, 'I don't need to see your identification.'

'These aren't the 'droids you're looking for,' Kenobi told him pleasantly.

'These aren't the 'droids we're looking for.'

'He can go about his business.'

'You can go about your business,' the metal-masked officer informed Luke.

'Move along,' Kenobi whispered.

'Move along,' the officer instructed Luke.

Unable to decide whether he should salute, nod, or give thanks to the man, Luke settled for nudging the accelerator. The landspeeder moved forward, drawing away from the circle of troops.

He peered up at his tall companion and started to say something. Kenobi only shook his head slowly and smiled. Swallowing his curiosity, Luke concentrated on guiding the speeder through steadily narrowing streets.

Luke studied the run-down structures and equally unwholesome-looking individuals they were passing. They had entered the oldest section of Mos Eisley where the old vices flourished most strongly.

Kenobi pointed and Luke pulled the landspeeder up in front of one of the original spaceport's first blockhouses. It had been converted into a cantina whose clientele was suggested by the diverse nature of transport parked outside. Some of them Luke recognised, others he had only heard rumours of.

Luke's mind was full of their narrow escape. 'I still can't understand how we got by those troops. I thought we were as good as dead.'

'The force is in the mind, Luke, and can sometimes be used to influence others. It's a powerful ally. You will discover that it can also be a danger.'

·Nodding without understanding, Luke indicated the run-down though obviously popular cantina. 'Do you really think we can find a pilot here capable of taking us all the way to Alderaan?'

Kenobi was exiting from the speeder. 'Most of the good, independent freighter pilots frequent this place, though many can afford better. They can talk freely here. Watch yourself, though. This place can be rough.'

Luke found himself squinting as they entered the cantina. It was darker inside than he would have liked. It didn't occur to him that the dim interior in combination with the brilliantly lit entrance permitted everyone inside to see each newcomer before he could see them.

Moving inward, Luke was astonished at the variety of beings making use of the bar. There were one-eyed creatures and thousand-eyed, creatures with scales, creatures with fur, and some with skin that seemed to ripple and change consistency according to their feelings.

Hovering near the bar itself was a towering insectoid that Luke glimpsed only as a threatening shadow. It contrasted with two of the tallest women Luke had ever seen. They were among the most normal-looking of the outrageous assemblage of humans that mixed freely among alien counterparts. Tentacles, claws, and hands were wrapped around drinking utensils of various sizes and shapes. Conversation was a steady babble of human and alien tongues.

Leaning close, Kenobi gestured towards the far end of the bar. A small knot of rough-looking humans lounged there, drinking, laughing, and trading stories of dubious origin.

'Corellians – pirates, most likely.'

'I thought we were looking for an independent freighter captain with his own ship for hire,' Luke whispered back.

'So we are, young Luke,' agreed Kenobi. 'And there's bound to be one or two adequate for our needs among that ground. It's just that in Corellian terminology the distinction between who owns what cargo tends to get a little muddled from time to time. Wait here.'

Luke nodded and watched as Kenobi worked his way through the crowd. The Corellians' suspicion at his approach vanished as soon as he engaged them in conversation.

Trying to maintain an air of quiet confidence, he returned his gaze to old Ben, and started when he saw what the oldster was talking to now. The Corellian was gone. In its place Kenobi was chatting with a towering anthropoid that showed a mouthful of teeth when it smiled.

Luke had heard about Wookiees, but he had never expected to see one. Despite an almost comical quasi-monkey face, the Wookiee was anything but gentle-looking. Only the large, glowing yellow eyes softened its otherwise awesome appearance. The massive torso was covered entirely with soft, thick russet fur. Less appealing cover consisted of a pair of chromed bandoliers which held lethal projectiles of a type unknown to Luke. Other than these, the Wookiees wore little.

Ben was talking to the Wookiee in its own language, quarrelling and hooting softly like a native. In the course of the conversation the old man had occasion to gesture in Luke's direction. Once the huge anthropoid stared directly at Luke and let out a horrifying howling laugh.

Disgruntled by the role he was evidently playing, Luke turned away and pretended to ignore the whole conversation. He might be acting unfairly towards the

68

creature, but he doubted that spine-quaking laugh was meant in gentle good-fellowship.

He couldn't understand what Ben wanted with the monster, or why he was spending his time in guttural conversation with it instead of with the now-vanished Corellians. So he sat and sipped his drink in silence, his eyes roving over the crowd in hopes of meeting a responsive gaze that held no belligerence.

Suddenly, something shoved him roughly from behind. He turned angrily, but his fury spent itself in astonishment. He found himself confronted by a large squarish monstrosity of multiple eyes and indeterminate origin.

'Negola dewaghi wooldugger!' the apparition bubbled challengingly.

Luke had never seen its like before; he knew neither its species nor its language. But he could tell by the way the creature bobbed and wove unsteadily on its podal supports that it had imbibed too much of whatever it considered a pleasing intoxicant.

Luke tried turning back to his own drink, studiously ignoring the creature. As he did so, a thing – a cross between a capybara and a small baboon – bounced over to squat next to the quivering many-eye. A short, grubby-looking human also approached and put a companionable arm around the snuffling mass.

'He doesn't like you,' the stubby human informed Luke in a surprisingly deep voice.

'I'm sorry about that.' Luke wished heartily he were somewhere else.

'I don't like you, either,' the smiling little man went on with brotherly negativity.

'I said I was sorry about it.'

' "Sorry," ' the human mimicked derisively. 'Are you insulting us? You just better watch yourself. We're all wanted.' He indicated his drunken companions. 'I have the death sentence on me in twelve different systems.'

At this the rodent let out a loud grunt. It was either a signal or a warning, because everything which had been leaning up at the bar immediately backed away, leaving a clear space around Luke and his antagonists.

Trying to salvage the situation, Luke essayed a wan smile. That faded rapidly when he saw that the three were readying hand weapons.

'This little one isn't worth the trouble,' a calm voice said. Luke looked up, startled. He hadn't heard Kenobi come up alongside him. 'Come, let me buy you all something . . . '

By way of reply the bulky monster chittered hideously and swung out a massive limb. It caught an unprepared Luke across the temple and sent him spinning across the room, crashing through tables and shattering a large jug filled with a foul-smelling liquid.

The crowd edged back farther, as the drunken monstrosity pulled a wicked-looking pistol from its service pouch. He started to wave it in Kenobi's direction.

That spurred the heretofore neutral bartender to life. 'No blasters, no blasters! Not in my place!'

The rodent thing chattered threateningly at him, while the weapon-wielding many-eye spared him a warning grunt.

In the split second when the gun and its owner's attention was off him, the old man's hand had moved to the disc slung at his side. The short human started to yell as a fiery blue-white light appeared in the dimness of the cantina.

He never finished the yell. It turned into a blink. When the blink was finished, the man found himself lying prone against the bar, moaning and whimpering as he stared at the stump of an arm.

In between the start of his yell and the conclusion of the blink, the rodent-thing had been cleft cleanly in half down the middle, its two halves falling in opposite directions. The giant multiocular creature still stood staring, dazed, at the old human who was poised motionless before it, the shining lightsabre held over his head. The creature's chrome pistol fired once, blowing a hole in the door. Then the torso peeled away as neatly as had

70

the body of the rodent, its two cauterised sections falling in opposite directions to lie motionless on the cool stone.

Only then did the suggestion of a sigh escape from Kenobi. Bringing the lightsabre down, he flipped it carefully upward in a reflex saluting motion which ended with the deactivated weapon resting innocuously on his hip.

To all appearances the cantina had returned to its former state, with one small exception. Ben Kenobi was given a respectful amount of space at the bar.

Luke was still shaken by the speed of the fight and by the old man's unimagined abilities. As his mind cleared and he moved to rejoin Kenobi, he could overhear bits and snatches of the talk around him. Much of it centred on admiration for the cleanness and finality of the fight.

'You're hurt, Luke,' Kenobi observed solicitously.

Luke felt of the bruise where the big creature had struck him. 'I . . . ' he started to say, but old Ben cut him off. He indicated the great hairy mass which was shouldering its way through the crowd towards them.

'This is Chewbacca,' he explained when the anthropoid joined them at the bar. 'He's first mate on a ship that might suit our needs. He'll take us to her captain-owner now.'

In front of the cantina, Threepio paced nervously next to the landspeeder. Apparently unconcerned, Artoo Detoo was engaged in animated electronic conversation with a bright red R-2 unit belonging to another of the cantina's patrons.

'What could be taking them so long? They went to hire one ship – not a fleet.'

Abruptly Threepio paused, beckoning silently to Artoo to be quiet. Two Imperial troopers had appeared on the scene. They were met by an unkempt human who had emerged from the depths of the cantina.

'I do not like the looks of this,' the tall 'droid murmured.

*

71

In a rear booth they encountered a sharp-featured young man perhaps five years older than Luke. He displayed the openness of the utterly confident – or the insanely reckless.

The Wookiee Chewbacca rumbled something at the man, and he nodded in response, glancing up at the newcomers pleasantly.

'You're pretty handy with that sabre, old man. Not often does one see that kind of swordplay in this part of the Empire anymore. I'm Han Solo, captain of the *Millennium Falcon*. (Suddenly he became all business.) 'Chewie tells me you're looking for passage to the Alderaan system?'

'That's right, son. If it's on a fast ship,' Kenobi told him.

'Fast ship? You mean you've never *heard* of the *Millennium Falcon*?'

Kenobi appeared amused. 'Should I?'

'It's the ship that made the Kessel run in less than twelve standard timeparts!' Solo told him indignantly. 'I've outrun Imperial starships and Corellian cruisers. What's your cargo?'

'Only passengers. Myself, the boy, and two 'droids – no questions asked.'

'No questions.' Solo looked up. 'Is it local trouble?'

'Let's just say we'd like to avoid any Imperial entanglements,' Kenobi replied.

'These days that can be a real trick. It'll cost you a little extra.' He did some mental figuring. 'All in all, about ten thousand. In advance.'

Luke gaped at the pilot. 'Ten thousand! We could almost buy our own ship for that.'

Solo shrugged. 'Maybe you could, but could you fly it?'

'You bet I could,' Luke shot back, rising. 'I'm not such a bad pilot myself. I don't – '

Again the firm hand on his arm. 'We haven't that much with us,' Kenobi explained. 'But we could pay you two thousand now, plus another fifteen when we reach Alderaan.'

Solo leaned forward uncertainly. 'Fifteen . . . You can really get your hands on that kind of money?'

'I promise it – from the government on Alderaan itself.'

'Seventeen thousand . . . All right, I'll chance it. You've got yourselves a ship. As for avoiding Imperial entanglements, you'd better twist out of here or even the *Millennium Falcon* won't be any help to you.' He nodded toward the entrance, and added quickly, 'Docking bay ninety-four, first thing in the morning.'

Four Imperial troopers, their eyes darting rapidly from table to booth to bar, had entered the cantina. Moving to the bar, the officer in charge asked the bartender a couple of brief questions. The big man hesitated a moment, then pointed towards a place near the back of the room. As he did so, his eyes widened slightly.

The booth he was pointing to was empty.

SEVEN

From their vantage point in another booth, Solo and Chewbacca watched as the Imperials strode through the bar. Two of them gave the Corellian a lingering glance. Chewbacca growled and the two soldiers hurried their pace.

Solo grinned sardonically, turning to his partner. 'Chewie, this charter could save our necks. Seventeen thousand!' He shook his head in amazement. 'Those two must really be desperate. I wonder what they're wanted for. Let's get going – the *Falcon* won't check itself out.'

'Going somewhere, Solo?'

The Corellian couldn't identify the voice, coming as it did through an electronic translator. But there was no problem recognising the speaker or the gun it held stuck in Solo's side.

The creature was roughly man-sized and bipedal, but it had huge, dull-faceted eyes, bulbous on a pea-green face. A ridge of short spines crested the high skull, while nostrils and mouth were contained in a tapirlike snout.

'As a matter of fact,' Solo replied slowly, 'I was just on my way to see your boss. You can tell Jabba I've got the money I owe him.'

'That's what you said yesterday – and last week – and the week prior to that. It's too late, Solo. I'm not going back to Jabba with another one of your stories.'

'But I've really got the money this time!' Solo protested.

'Fine. I'll take it now, please.'

Solo sat down slowly. Jabba's minions were apt to be cursed with nervous trigger fingers. The alien took the seat across from him, the muzzle of the ugly little pistol never straying from Solo's chest.

'I haven't got it here with me. Tell Jabba –',

'It's too late, I think. Jabba would rather have your ship.'

'Over my dead body,' Solo said unamiably.

The alien was not impressed. 'If you insist. Will you come outside with me, or must I finish it here?'

Light and noise filled the little corner of the cantina, and when it had faded, all that remained of the unctuous alien was a smoking, slimy spot on the stone floor.

Solo brought his hand and the smoking weapon it held from beneath the table, drawing bemused stares from several of the cantina's patrons. They had known the creature had committed its fatal mistake in allowing Solo the chance to get his hands under cover.

Leaving the booth, Solo flipped the bartender a handful of coins as he and Chewbacca moved off. 'Sorry for the mess. I always was a rotten host.'

'They're starting to search the spaceport central,' the

Commander declared, having to alternately run and then walk to keep pace with the long strides of Darth Vader. The Dark Lord was deep in thought as he strode down one of the battle station's main corridors, trailed by several aides.

'The reports are just starting to come in,' the Commander went on. 'It's only a matter of time before we have those 'droids.'

'Send in more men if you have to. Never mind the protests of the planetary Governor – I must have those 'droids. It's her hope of that data being used against us that is the pillar of her resistance to the mind probes.'

'I understand, Lord Vader. Until then we must waste our time with Governor Tarkin's foolish plan to break her.'

'There's docking bay ninety-four,' Luke told Kenobi and the robots, 'and there's Chewbacca. He seems excited about something.'

The big Wookiee was waving over the heads of the crowd and jabbering loudly in their direction. Speeding their pace, none of the foursome noticed the small, dark-clad thing that had followed them from the transporter lot.

The creature moved into the doorway and pulled a tiny transmitter from a pouch concealed by its multifold robes. The transmitter looked far too new and modern to be in the grasp of so decrepit a specimen, yet its manipulator was speaking into it with steady assurance.

Docking bay ninety-four, Luke noted, was no different in appearance from a host of other docking bays scattered throughout Mos Eisley. It consisted mostly of an entrance rampway and an enormous pit gouged from the rocky soil. This served as clearance radii for the effects of the simple antigrav drive which boosted all spacecraft clear of the gravitational field of the planet.

The mathematics of spacedrive were simple enough even to Luke. Antigrav could operate only when there was a sufficient gravity well to push against – like that

75

of a planet – whereas supralight travel could only take place when a ship was clear of that same gravity. Hence the necessity for the dual-drive system on any extra-system craft.

That battered ellipsoid which could only loosely be labelled a ship appeared to have been pieced together out of old hull fragments and components discarded as unusable by other craft.

'What a piece of junk,' he murmured, unable to hide his feelings. They were walking up the rampway towards the open port. 'This thing couldn't possibly make it into hyperspace.'

Kenobi didn't comment, but merely gestured towards the port, where a figure was coming to meet them.

Solo was used to the reaction the sight of the *Millennium Falcon* produced in prospective passengers. 'She may not look like much,' he confessed as he approached them, 'but she's all go. I've added a few unique modifications to her myself. In addition to piloting, I like to tinker. She'll make point five factors beyond lightspeed.'

Luke scratched his head as he tried to reassess the craft in view of its owner's claims. Either the Corellian was the biggest liar this side of the galactic centre, or there was more to this vessel than met the eye. Luke decided to reserve judgement on the ship and its pilot until after he had watched them in operation.

Chewbacca rushed up the ramp, a hairy whirlwind, and blabbered excitedly at Solo. The pilot regarded him coolly, nodding from time to time, then barked a brief reply. The Wookiee charged into the ship, pausing only to urge everyone to follow.

'We seem to be a bit rushed,' Solo explained cryptically, 'so if you'll hurry aboard, we'll be off.'

Inside, Luke was startled to see the bulky Chewbacca squirm and fight his way into a pilot's chair which was overwhelmed by his massive form. The Wookiee flipped several tiny switches with digits seemingly too big for the task. Those great paws drifted with surprising grace over the controls.

A deep throbbing started somewhere within the ship as the engines were activated. Luke and Ben began strapping themselves into the vacant seats in the main passageway.

Outside the docking-bay entrance a long, leathery snout protruded from dark folds of cloth, and somewhere in the depths to either side of that imposing proboscis, eyes stared intently. They turned as a squad of eight Imperial troops rushed up. They headed straight for the enigmatic figure who whispered something to the lead trooper and gestured to the docking bay.

The information must have been provocative. Activating their weapons and raising them to firing position, the troops charged en masse down the docking bay entrance.

A glint of light on moving metal caught Solo's eyes as the outlines of the first troops showed themselves. Several dropped to their knees and opened fire on him. Solo ducked back inside, turning to yell forward.

'Chewie – deflector shields, quick! Get us out of here!'

A throaty roar of acknowledgement came back to him.

Drawing his own pistol, Solo managed to snap off a couple of bursts from the comparative safety of the hatchway. The exposed troops dove for cover.

The low throbbing rose to a whine, then to a deafening howl as Solo's hand came down on the quick-release button. Immediately the overhead hatchcover slammed shut.

As the retreating troops raced out of the docking bay entrance, the ground was trembling steadily. They ran smack into a second squad, which had just arrived in response to the rapidly spreading emergency call. One of the soldiers explained to the newly arrived ranking officer what had happened back in the bay.

The officer whipped out a compact communicator

and shouted into it, 'Flight deck . . . they're trying to escape! Send everything you've got after this ship.'

All across Mos Eisley, alarms began to sound, spreading out from docking bay ninety-four in concentric circles of concern.

Several soldiers scouring one alleyway reacted to the citywide alarm at the same time as they saw the small freighter lift gracefully into the clear blue sky. It shrank to a pinpoint before any of them thought to bring a weapon to bear.

Luke and Ben were already undoing their acceleration straps as Solo walked past them, towards the cockpit. He sat in the pilot's seat and began checking readouts and gauges. Next to him Chewbacca turned from his own instruments to jab a massive finger at the tracking screen.

Solo gave it a quick glance, then turned irritably to his own panel. 'Looks like two, maybe three destroyers. Try to hold them off until I can finish the programming for the supralight jump. Angle the deflectors for maximum shielding.' His hands flew over the computer input terminals.

Rear scanners showed the baleful lemon eye of Tatooine shrinking rapidly behind them. It wasn't rapid enough to eliminate the three points of light that indicated the pursuing Imperial warships.

Solo turned to acknowledge the entrance of his human passengers. 'We've got two more coming in from different angles,' he told them, scrutinising the instrumentation. 'They're going to try to box up before we can jump. Five ships . . . What did you two do to attract that kind of company?'

'Can't you outrun them?' Luke asked sarcastically, 'I thought you said this thing was fast.'

'Watch your mouth, kid, or you'll find yourself floating home. There's too many of 'em, for one thing. But, we'll be safe enough once we've made the jump into hyperspace.' He grinned knowingly. 'Can't nobody

78

track another ship accurately at supralight speeds. Plus, I know a few tricks that ought to lose any persistent stick-tights.'

Luke had a retort poised on his lips. It was wiped out as he threw up his arms to ward off a brilliant red flash which gave black space outside the viewport the temporary aspect of the surface of a sun. Kenobi, Solo, and even Chewbacca did likewise, since the proximity of the explosion nearly overrode the phototropic shielding.

'Here's where the situation gets interesting,' Solo muttered.

'How long before you can make the jump?' Kenobi inquired.

'We're still within the gravitational influence of Tatooine,' came the cool response. 'It will be a few minutes yet before the navigation computer can compensate and effect an accurate jump. I could override its decision, but the hyperdrive would likely shred itself.'

'A few minutes,' Luke blurted, staring at the screens. 'At the rate they're gaining . . .'

'Travelling through hyperspace isn't like dusting crops, boy. Ever tried calculating a hyperspace jump?' Luke had to shake his head. 'It's no mean trick. Be nice if we rushed it and passed right through a star or some other friendly spatial phenom like a black hole. That would end our trip real quick.'

Fresh explosions continued to flare close by despite Chewbacca's best efforts at evasion. On Solo's console a red warning light began to flash for attention.

'What's that?' Luke wondered nervously.

'We're losing a deflector shield,' Solo informed him. 'Better strap yourselves back in. We're almost ready to make the jump.'

Back in the main hold area Threepio was already locked tightly into his seat by metal arms stronger than any acceleration straps. Artoo swayed back and forth under the concussion produced by increasingly powerful energy bursts against the ship's deflectors.

'Was this trip really necessary?' the tall robot muttered in desperation. 'I'd forgotten how much I hate space travel.'

Admiral Motti entered the quiet conference room. His gaze went to Governor Tarkin. He bowed slightly, and announced, 'We have entered the Alderaan system. We await your order.'

The door slid aside and Leia Organa entered, flanked by two armed guards, followed by Darth Vader.

'I am – ' Tarkin began.

'I know who you are,' she spat, 'Governor Tarkin. I should have expected to find you holding Vader's leash. I thought I recognised your unique stench when I was first brought on board.'

'Lord Vader has informed me that your resistance to our traditional methods of inquiry – ' Tarkin began.

'Torture, you mean,' she countered a trifle shakily. 'I'm surprised you had the courage to take the responsibility for issuing the order on yourself.'

Tarkin sighed. 'Before your execution I should like you to be my guest at a small ceremony. It will certify this battle station's operational status, at the same time ushering in a new era of Imperial technical supremacy. This station is the final link in the new-forged Imperial chain which will bind the million systems of the galactic Empire together once and for all. Your petty Alliance will no longer be of any concern to us. After today's demonstration no one will dare to oppose Imperial decree, not even the Senate.'

Organa looked at him with contempt. 'Force will not keep the Empire together. Force has never kept anything together for very long. The more you tighten your grip, the more systems will slip through your fingers. You're a foolish man, Governor. Foolish men often choke to death on their own delusions.'

Tarkin smiled a death's head smile. 'It will be interesting to see what manner of passing Lord Vader has in mind for you. I am certain it will be worthy of you – and of him.

'You have determined the choice of subject for this demonstration. Since you have proven reluctant to supply us with the location of the rebel stronghold, I have deemed it appropriate to select as an alternate subject your home planet of Alderaan.'

'No! You can't! Alderaan is a peaceful world, with no standing armies. You can't . . . '

Tarkin's eyes gleamed. 'You would prefer another target? For the last time, where is the main rebel base?'

A voice announced over a hidden speaker that they had approached within antigrav range of Alderaan – approximately six planetary diameters. That was enough to accomplish what all of Vader's infernal devices had failed to.

'Dantooine,' she whispered, all defiance gone. 'They're on Dantooine.'

Tarkin let out a slow sigh of satisfaction, then turned to the black figure nearby. 'You see, Lord Vader? She can be reasonable. One needs only frame the question properly to elicit the desired response.' He directed his attention to the other officers. 'After concluding our little test here we shall make haste to move on to Dantooine. You may proceed with the operation, gentlemen.'

It took several seconds for Tarkin's words to penetrate. *'What!'* Organa finally gasped.

'Dantooine,' Tarkin explained, examining his fingers, 'is too far from the centres of Imperial population to serve as the subject of an effective demonstration. For reports of our power to spread rapidly through the Empire we require an obstreperous world more centrally located. Have no fear, though. We will deal with your rebel friends on Dantooine as soon as possible.'

'But you said . . . ' Organa started to protest.

He gestured to the two soldiers flanking her. 'Escort her to the principal observation level and,' he smiled, 'make certain she is provided with an unobstructed view.'

EIGHT

Solo was busily checking readouts from gauges and dials in the hold area. Occasionally he would pass a small box across various sensors, study the result, and cluck with pleasure.

'You can stop worrying about your Imperial friends,' he told Luke and Ben. 'They'll never be able to track us now. Told you I'd lose them.'

Kenobi might have nodded briefly in response, but he was engaged in explaining something to Luke.

'Don't everybody thank me at once,' Solo grunted. 'Anyway, navigation computer calculates our arrival in Alderaan orbit at oh-two-hundred.'

Luke stood frozen in the middle of the hold. He held an activated lightsabre in position over his head. A low hum came from the ancient instrument while Luke lunged and parried under Ben Kenobi's instructive gaze.

'No Luke, your cuts should flow, not be so choppy,' Kenobi instructed gently. 'Remember, the force is omnipresent. It envelops you as it radiates from you. A Jedi warrior can actually feel the force as a physical thing.'

'It is an energy field, then?' Luke inquired.

'It is an energy field and something more,' Kenobi went on. 'An aura that at once controls and obeys. It is a nothingness that can accomplish miracles.' He looked thoughtful for a moment.

'No one, not even the Jedi scientists, were able to truly define the force. Possibly no one ever will. Sometimes there is as much magic as science in the explanations of the force. Yet what is a magician but a practising theorist? Now, let's try again.'

The old man was hefting a silvery globe about the size of a man's fist. It was covered with fine antennae, some as delicate as those of a moth. He flipped it toward

Luke and watched as it halted a couple of metres away from the boy's face.

Luke readied himself as the ball circled him slowly, turning to face it as it assumed a new position. Abruptly it executed a lightning-swift lunge, only to freeze about a metre away. Luke failed to succumb to the feint, and the ball soon backed off.

Moving slowly to one side in an effort to get around the ball's fore sensors, Luke drew the sabre back preparatory to striking. As he did so the ball darted in behind *him*. A thin pencil of red light jumped from one of the antennae to the back of Luke's thigh, knocking him to the deck even as he was bringing his sabre around – too late.

Rubbing at his tingling, sleeping leg, Luke tried to ignore the burst of accusing laughter from Solo. 'Hocus-pocus religions and archaic weapons are no substitute for a good blaster at your side,' the pilot sneered.

'You don't believe in the force?' asked Luke, struggling back to his feet.

'I've been from one end of this galaxy to the other,' the pilot boasted, 'and I've seen a lot of strange things. Too many to believe there couldn't be something like this "force". Too many to think that there could be some such controlling one's actions. *I* determine my destiny – not some half-mystical energy field.' He gestured towards Kenobi. 'I wouldn't follow him so blindly, if I were you. He's a clever old man, full of simple tricks and mischief. He might be using you for his own ends.'

Kenobi only smiled gently, then turned back to face Luke. 'I suggest you try it again, Luke,' he said. 'You must try to divorce your actions from conscious control. Try not to focus on anything concrete, visually or mentally. You must let your mind drift; only then can you use the force. You have to enter a state in which you act on what you sense, not on what you think beforehand. You must cease cogitation, relax, stop thinking . . . let yourself drift . . . free . . . free . . . '

The old man's voice had dropped to a mesmerising buzz. As he finished, the chrome bulb darted at Luke. Dazed by Kenobi's hypnotic tone, Luke didn't see it charge. But as the ball neared, he whirled with amazing speed, the sabre arcing up and out in a peculiar fashion. The red beam that the globe emitted was neatly deflected to one side. Its humming stopped and the ball bounced to the deck, all animation gone.

Blinking as if coming awake from a short nap, Luke stared in absolute astonishment at the inert remote.

'You see, you can do it,' Kenobi told him. 'One can teach only so much. Now you must learn to admit the force when you want it, so that you can learn to control it consciously.'

Moving to one side, Kenobi took a large helmet from behind a locker and walked over to Luke. Placing the helmet over his head effectively eliminated the boy's vision.

'I can't see,' Luke muttered, turning around and forcing Kenobi to step back out of range of the dangerously wavering sabre. 'How can I fight?'

'With the force,' old Ben explained. 'You didn't really "see" the seeker when it went for your legs the last time, and yet you parried its beam. Try to let that sensation flow within you again.'

'I *can't* do it,' Luke moaned. 'I'll get hit again.'

'Not if you let yourself trust *you*,' Kenobi insisted. 'This is the only way to be certain you're relying wholly on the force.'

Bending over the chrome globe, he touched a control at its side. Then he tossed it straight up. It arched towards Luke. Braking in midfall, the ball plummeted stonelike towards the deck. Luke swung the sabre at it. While it was a commendable try, it wasn't nearly fast enough. Once again the little antenna glowed. This time the crimson needle hit Luke square on the seat of his pants. Luke let out a yelp of pain as he spun, trying to strike his invisible tormentor.

'Relax!' old Ben urged him. 'Be free. You're trying

84

to use your eyes and ears. Stop predicting and use the rest of your mind.'

Suddenly the youth stopped, wavering slightly. The seeker was still behind him. Changing direction again, it made another dive and fired.

Simultaneously the lightsabre jerked around, as accurate as it was awkward in its motion, to deflect the bolt. This time the ball didn't fall motionless to the deck. Instead it backed up three metres and remained there, hovering.

Aware that the drone of the remote seeker no longer assaulted his ears, a cautious Luke peeked out from under the helmet. Sweat and exhaustion competed for space on his face.

'Did I – ?'

'I told you you could,' Kenobi informed him with pleasure. 'Once you start to trust your inner self there'll be no stopping you. I told you there was much of your father in you.'

'I'd call it luck,' snorted Solo as he concluded his examination of the readouts.

As he was speaking a small telltale light on the far side of the hold had begun flashing. Chewbacca noticed it and called out to him.

Solo glanced at the board, then informed his passengers, 'We're coming up on Alderaan. We'll be slowing down shortly and going back under lightspeed. Come on, Chewie.'

The Wookiee followed his partner towards the cockpit. Luke watched them depart, but his mind wasn't on their imminent arrival at Alderaan. It was burning with something that seemed to grow and mature at the back of his brain as he dwelt on it.

'You know,' he murmured, 'I did feel something. I could almost "see" the outlines of the remote.' He gestured at the hovering device behind him.

Kenobi's voice when he replied was solemn. 'Luke, you've taken the first step into a larger universe.'

Dozens of humming, buzzing instruments lent the

freighter's cockpit the air of a busy hive. Solo and Chewbacca had their attention locked on the most vital of those instruments.

'Steady . . . stand by, Chewie.' Solo adjusted several manual compensators. 'Ready to go sublight . . . ready . . . cut us in, Chewie.'

The Wookiee turned something on the console before him. At the same time Solo pulled back on a comparatively large lever. Abruptly the long streaks of Doppler-distorted starlight slowed to hyphen shapes, then finally to familiar bolts of fire. A gauge on the console registered zero.

Gigantic chunks of glowing stone appeared out of the nothingness, barely shunted aside by the ship's deflectors. The strain caused the *Millennium Falcon* to begin shuddering violently.

'What the – ?' Next to him, Chewbacca flipped off several controls and activated others. Only the fact that Solo always emerged from supralight travel with his deflectors up – just in case any unfriendly folk might be waiting for him – had saved the freighter from instant destruction.

Luke fought to keep his balance as he made his way into the cockpit. 'What's going on?'

'We're back in normal space,' Solo informed him, 'but we've come out in the middle of the worst asteroid storm I've ever seen. It's not on any of our charts.' He peered hard at several indicators. 'According to the galactic atlas, our position is correct. Only one thing is missing: Alderaan.'

'Missing? But – that's crazy!'

'Look for yourself. I've triple-checked the co-ordinates, and there's nothing wrong with the nav 'puter. We ought to be standing out one planetary diameter from the surface. The planet's glow should be filling the cockpit, but – there's nothing out there. Nothing but debris.' He paused. 'Judging from the level of wild energy outside and the amount of solid waste, I'd guess that Alderaan's been . . . blown away. Totally.'

'Destroyed,' Luke whispered, overwhelmed at the spectre raised by such an unimaginable disaster. 'But – how?'

'The Empire,' a voice declared firmly. Ben Kenobi had come in behind Luke, and his attention was held by the emptiness ahead as well as the import behind it.

'No.' Solo was shaking his head slowly. Even he was stunned by the enormity of what the old man was suggesting. That a human agency had been responsible for the annihilation of an entire population, of a planet itself . . .

'No . . . the entire Imperial fleet couldn't have done this. It would take a thousand ships massing a lot more firepower than has ever existed.'

Muffled alarms began humming loudly as a synchronous light flashed on the control console. Solo bent to the instrumentation.

'Another ship,' he announced. 'Can't judge the type yet.'

'A survivor, maybe – someone who might know what happened,' Luke ventured hopefully.

Ben Kenobi's next words shattered that hope. 'That's an Imperial fighter.'

Chewbacca suddenly gave an angry bark. A huge flower of destruction blossomed outside the port, battering the freighter violently. A tiny, double-winged ball raced past the cockpit port.

'It followed us!' Luke shouted.

'From Tatooine? It couldn't have,' objected a disbelieving Solo. 'Not in hyperspace.'

Kenobi was studying the configuration the tracking screen displayed. 'You're quite right, Han. It's the short-range Tie fighter.'

'But where did it come from?' the Corellian wanted to know. 'There are no Imperial bases near here. It couldn't have been a Tie job.'

'You saw it pass.'

'I know. It looked like a Tie fighter – but what about a base?'

'It's leaving in a big hurry,' Luke noted, studying the tracker. 'If it identifies us we're in big trouble.'

'Not if I can help it,' Solo declared. 'Chewie, jam its transmission. Lay in a pursuit course.'

'It's already too far out of range,' Kenobi ventured thoughtfully.

'Not for long.'

All eyes were on the tracking screen and viewport. At first the Imperial fighter tried a complex evasive course, to no avail. The surprisingly manoeuvrable freighter hung tight on its tail, continuing to make up the distance between them. Seeing that he couldn't shake his pursuers, the fighter pilot had opened up his tiny engine all the way.

Ahead, one of the multitude of stars was becoming steadily brighter. Luke frowned. They were moving fast, but not nearly fast enough for any heavenly object to brighten so rapidly. Something here didn't make sense.

The star ahead continued to brighten, its glow evidently coming from within. It assumed a circular outline.

'He's heading for that small moon,' Luke murmured.

'The Empire must have an outpost there,' Solo admitted. 'Although according to the atlas, Alderaan had no moons. But I think I can get him before he gets there; he's almost in range.'

They drew steadily nearer. Gradually craters and mountains on the moon became visible. Yet there was something extremely odd about them. The craters were far too regular in outline, the mountains far too vertical, canyons and valleys impossibly straight and regularised.

'That's no moon,' Kenobi breathed softly. 'That's a space station.'

'But it's too big,' Solo objected. 'It can't be artificial – it can't!'

Abruptly the usually calm Kenobi was shouting. 'Turn the ship around! Let's get out of here!'

'You're right, old man. Full reverse, Chewie.'

The Wookiee started adjusting controls, and the freighter seemed to slow, arcing around in a broad curve. The tiny fighter leaped instantly towards the monstrous station until it was swallowed up by its overpowering bulk.

'Lock in auxiliary power!' Solo ordered.

Gauges began to whine in protest, and by ones and twos every instrument on the control console went berserk. Try as he might, Solo couldn't keep the surface of the gargantuan station from looming steadily larger.

Luke stared wildly at secondary installations as big as mountains, dish antennae larger than all of Mos Eisley. 'Why are we still moving towards it?'

'We're caught in a tractor beam – strongest one I ever saw. It's dragging us in,' the pilot muttered.

'You mean, there's nothing you can do?' Luke asked, feeling unbelievably helpless.

Solo studied the overloaded sensor readouts and shook his head. 'Not against this kind of power. I'm on full power myself, kid, and it's not shifting out of course a fraction of a degree. It's no use. I'm going to have to shut down or we'll melt our engines. But they're not going to suck me up without a fight!'

He started to vacate the pilot's chair, but was restrained by an aged yet powerful hand on his shoulder. 'If it's a fight you cannot win – well, my boy, there are always alternatives to fighting ...'

The true size of the battle station became apparent as the freighter was pulled closer and closer. Running around the station's equator was an artificial cluster of metal mountains, docking ports stretching beckoning fingers nearly two kilometres above the surface.

Now only a minuscule speck against the grey bulk of the station, the *Millenium Falcon* was sucked towards one of those steel pseudopods and finally swallowed by it. A lake of metal closed off the entryway, and the freighter vanished as if it had never existed.

*

Vader stared at the motley array of stars displayed on the conference-room map. Interestingly, the first use of the most powerful destructive machine ever constructed had seemingly had no influence at all on that map, which represented only a tiny fraction of this section of one modest-sized galaxy.

It would take a microbreakdown of a portion of this map to reveal a slight reduction in spatial mass, caused by the disappearance of Alderaan. Alderaan, with its many cities, farms, factories, and towns – and traitors, Vader reminded himself.

Despite his advances and intricate technological methods of annihilation, the actions of mankind remained unnoticeable to an uncaring, unimaginably vast universe. If Vader's grandest plans ever came to pass, all that would change.

Despite all their intelligence and drive, the vastness and wonder were lost on the two men who continued to chatter behind him. Tarkin and Motti were talented and ambitious, but they saw things only on the scale of human pettiness.

Still, neither man was a Dark Lord. Little more could be expected of them. These two were useful now but someday they, like Alderaan, would have to be swept aside. For now he could not afford to ignore them. He would have preferred the company of equals, but, at this point, he *had* no equals.

He turned to them. 'The defence systems on Alderaan, despite the Senator's protestations to the contrary, were as strong as any in the Empire. Our demonstration was as impressive as it was thorough.'

Tarkin turned to him, nodding. 'The Senate is being informed of our action at this very moment. Soon we will be able to announce the extermination of the Alliance itself, as soon as we have dealt with their main military base. Now that their main source of munitions, Alderaan, has been eliminated, the rest of those systems with secessionist inclinations will fall in line quickly enough, you'll see.'

Tarkin turned as an Imperial officer entered the chamber. 'Yes, what is it, Cass?'

'Governor, the advance scouts have reached and circumnavigated Dantooine. They have found the remains of a rebel base . . . which they estimate has been deserted for some time. Years, possibly. They are proceeding with an extensive survey of the remainder of the system.'

Tarkin turned apoplectic. 'She lied! She lied to us!'

Vader smiled behind his mask. 'I told you she would never betray the rebellion – unless she thought her confession could somehow destroy us in the process.'

'Terminate her immediately!' The Governor was barely able to form words.

'Calm yourself, Tarkin,' Vader advised him. 'She can still be of value to us.'

'You just said it yourself, Vader: we'll get nothing more out of her. I'll find that hidden fortress if I have to destroy every star system in this sector. I'll – '

A quiet yet demanding beep interrupted him.

'Yes, what is it?' he inquired irritably.

A voice reported over an unseen speaker. 'Sirs, we've captured a small freighter that was entering the remains of Alderaan. A standard check indicates that its markings match that of the ship which blasted its way out of quarantine at Mos Eisley, Tatooine system, and went hyper before the Imperial blockade craft there could close on it.'

Tarkin looked puzzled. 'Mos Eisley? Tatooine? What is this? What's this all about, Vader?'

'It means, Tarkin, that the last of our unresolved difficulties is about to be eliminated. Someone apparently received the missing data tapes, learned who transcribed them, and was trying to return them to her. We may be able to facilitate their meeting with the Senator.'

Tarkin nodded. 'I leave this matter in your hands, Vader.'

*

The freighter sat listlessly in the docking hangar of the huge bay. Thirty armed Imperial troopers stood before the lowered main ramp leading into the ship. They snapped to attention when Vader and a Commander approached. Vader halted at the base of the ramp, studying the vessel as an officer came forward.

'There was no reply to our repeated signals, sir, so we activated the ramp from outside. We've made no contact with anyone aboard either by communicator or in person,' the officer reported.

'Send your men in,' Vader ordered.

Turning, the officer relayed the command to a non-com, who barked orders. A number of the heavily armoured soldiers made their way up the ramp and entered the outer hold.

Inside, two men covered a third as he advanced. Moving in groups of three in this fashion, they rapidly spread through the ship. Corridors rang hollowly under metal-shod feet, and doors slid aside willingly as they were activated.

'Empty,' the Sergeant in charge finally declared in surprise. 'Check the cockpit.'

Several troopers made their way forward and slid the portal aside, only to discover the pilot's chairs as vacant as the rest of the freighter. The controls were deactivated and all systems shut down. Only a single light on the console winked on and off fitfully. The Sergeant moved forward, recognised the source of the light, and activated the appropriate controls. A printout appeared on a nearby screen. He studied it intently, then turned to convey the information to his superior, who was waiting by the main hatch.

That worthy listened carefully before he turned and called down to the Commander and Vader. 'There is no one aboard; the ship is completely deserted, sirs. According to the ship's log, her crew abandoned ship immediately after lift-off, then set her on automatics for Alderaan.'

Vader hesitated before replying. 'This doesn't feel

right. Send a fully equipped scanning team on board. I want every centimetre of that ship checked out. See to it as soon as possible.' With that, he whirled and stalked from the hangar, sure that he was overlooking something of vital importance.

Below, the muffled sounds of the officer giving final orders faded, leaving the interior in complete quiet. The quivering of a portion of the floor was the only movement on board.

Abruptly the quivering became a sharp upheaval. Two metal panels popped upward, followed by a pair of tousled heads. Han Solo and Luke looked around quickly, then managed to relax a little when it became clear that the ship was empty.

'Lucky you'd built these compartments,' Luke commented.

'Where did you think I kept smuggled goods – in the main hold? I admit I never expected to smuggle myself in them.' He started violently at a sudden sound, but it was only another panel shifting aside.

'This is ridiculous. It isn't going to work. Even if I could take off and get past the closed hatch' – he jabbed a thumb upward – 'we'd never get past that tractor beam.'

Another panel opened, revealing the face of an elderly imp. 'You leave that to me.'

'I was afraid you'd say something like that,' muttered Solo.

Kenobi grinned at him. 'What does that say of the man who allows himself to be hired by a fool?'

Two technicians had arrived at the base of the ramp. They reported to the two bored soldiers guarding it.

'The ship's all yours,' one of the troopers told them. 'If the scanners pick up anything, report it immediately.'

The men nodded, then strained to lug their heavy equipment up the ramp. As soon as they disappeared inside, a loud crash was heard. Both guards whirled,

93

then heard a voice call, 'Hey, down there, could you give us a hand with this?'

One trooper looked at his companion, who shrugged. They both started up the ramp, muttering at the inefficiency of mere technicians. A second crashing sound reverberated, but now there was no one left to hear it.

But the absence of the two troopers *was* noticed. A gantry officer passing the window of a small command office near the freighter entrance glanced out, frowning when he saw no sign of the guards. Concerned but not alarmed, he moved to a comlink and spoke into it.

'THX-1138, why aren't you at your post? THX-1138, do you copy?'

The speaker gave back only static.

'THX-1138, why don't you reply?' The officer was beginning to panic when an armoured figure descended the ramp. Pointing to his helmet, the figure tapped it to indicate the comlink wasn't working.

Shaking his head in disgust, the gantry officer gave his busy aide an annoyed look as he made for the door. 'Take over here. We've got another bad transmitter. I'm going to see what I can do.' He activated the door, took a step forward as it slid aside – and stumbled backward in a state of shock.

Filling the door completely was a towering hairy form. Chewbacca leaned inward and with a bone-splintering howl flattened the officer with one swipe of a pan-sized fist.

The aide was already on his feet and reaching for his sidearm when a narrow energy beam passed completely through him, piercing his heart. Solo followed the Wookiee into the room. Kenobi and the 'droids squeezed in behind him, with Luke, also clad in the armour of a luckless Imperial soldier, bringing up the rear.

Luke was looking around nervously as he shut the door behind them. 'Between his howling and your blasting everything in sight, it's a wonder the entire station doesn't know we're here.'

'Bring 'em on,' Solo demanded, unreasonably enthused by their success so far. 'I prefer a straight fight to all this sneaking around.'

'Maybe you're in a hurry to die,' Luke snapped, 'but I'm not. All this sneaking around has kept us alive.'

They watched as Kenobi operated an incredibly complex computer console with ease and confidence. A screen lit up promptly with a map of sections of the battle station. The old man leaned forward, scrutinising the display carefully.

Meanwhile, Threepio and Artoo had been going over an equally complicated control panel nearby. Artoo suddenly froze and began whistling wildly at something he had found. Solo and Luke rushed over to where the robots were standing. Chewbacca busied himself hanging the gantry officer up by his toes.

'Plug him in,' Kenobi suggested, looking over from his place before the larger readout. 'He should be able to draw information from the entire station network. Let's see if he can find out where the tractorbeam power unit is located.'

'Why not just disconnect the beam from here, sir?' Luke wanted to know.

It was Solo who replied derisively, 'What, and have them lock it right back on us before we can get a ship's length outside the docking bay?'

Luke looked crestfallen. 'Oh. I hadn't thought of that.'

'We have to break the tractor at its power source in order to execute a clean escape, Luke,' old Ben chided gently as Artoo punched a claw arm into the open computer socket he had discovered. Immediately a galaxy of lights came to life on the panel in front of him and the room was filled with the hum of machinery working at high speed.

Several minutes passed while the little 'droid sucked up information like a metal sponge. Then the hum slowed and he turned to beep something back at them.

'He's found it, sir!' Threepio announced excitedly.

'The tractor beam is coupled to the main reactors at seven locations. Most of the pertinent data is restricted, but he'll try to pull the critical information through to the monitor.'

Kenobi turned his attention from the larger screen to a small readout near Artoo. Data began to race across it too fast for Luke to see, but apparently Kenobi somehow made something of the schematic blur. 'I don't think there's any way you boys can help with this,' he told them. 'I must go alone.'

Luke wasn't put off so easily. 'I want to go with you.'

'Don't be impatient, young Luke. Stay and watch over the 'droids and wait for my signal. They must be delivered to the rebel forces or many more worlds will meet the same fate as Alderaan. Trust in the force, Luke – and wait.'

Kenobi adjusted the lightsabre at his waist. Stepping to the door, he slid it aside, and disappeared down a long, glowing hallway.

A hysterical whistling and hooting came from the computer console. Luke hurried over to Artoo Detoo.

'What now?' Luke asked Threepio.

The taller robot looked puzzled himself. 'I'm afraid I don't understand either, sir. He says, "I found her," and keeps repeating, "She's here, she's here!"'

'Who? Who has he found?'

Artoo whistled frantically.

'Princess Leia,' Threepio announced after listening carefully. 'Senator Organa – they seem to be one and the same. I believe she may be the person in the message he was carrying.'

That three-dimensional portrait of indescribable beauty coalesced in Luke's mind again. 'The Princess? She's here?'

Attracted by the commotion, Solo wandered over. 'Princess? What's going on?'

'Where? Where is she?' Luke demanded breathlessly, ignoring Solo completely.

Artoo whistled on while Threepio translated. 'Level

Stormtroopers are the drones of the Galactic Empire who carry out a reign of terror among the disheartened worlds of the galaxy. Hidden underneath white armored spacesuits, these fearsome troops enforce the restrictive laws with callous disregard for human rights. Quite often they are tools used to further the personal ambitions of the Imperial governors and bureaucrats.

An alliance of underground freedom fighters are challenging the tyranny and oppression of the awesome Galactic Empire. Idealists and adventurers from a small number of systems joined together to stop the growing outrages. Striking from a fortress hidden among the billion stars of the galaxy, rebel spaceships have been winning a growing number of victories.

Jawas

Tusken Raiders

Jawas are the meter-high creatures who travel the wastes of Tatooine collecting and selling scrap. They scurry about in a rodent-like manner in rough-hewn cloaks thickly coated with dust and sand. These overly cautious creatures jabber in low gutteral croaks and hisses. The shrouded creatures smell horribly, attracting small insects to the dark recesses where their mouths and nostrils should be.

Tusken Raiders, or Sandpeople as they are sometimes called, wear abundant clothing to protect themselves from Tatooine's twin suns. These large, strong creatures pursue a nomadic existence in some of Tatooine's most desolate regions. Vicious desert bandits, they fear little and make sudden raids on local settlers. They are marginally human creatures who are not to be trifled with.

five, detention block AA-23. According to the information, she is scheduled for slow termination.'

'What are you three blabbering about?' an exasperated Solo demanded.

'She's the one who programmed the message into Artoo Detoo,' Luke explained hurriedly, 'the one we were trying to deliver to Alderaan. We've got to help her.'

'Now, just a minute,' Solo cautioned him. 'When I said I didn't have any "better ideas" I meant it. The old man said to wait here. I'm not going off on some crazy maze through this place.'

'But Ben didn't know she was here,' Luke pleaded. 'I'm sure that if he knew he would have changed his plans. Now, if we could just figure a way to get into that detention block . . . '

Solo shook his head and stepped back. 'I'm not going into any Imperial detention blocks.'

'If we don't do something, they're going to execute her. A minute ago you said you didn't just want to sit here and wait to be captured. Now you want to stay. Which is it?'

The Corellian looked troubled – and confused. 'Marching into a detention area's not what I had in mind. We're likely to end up there anyway – why rush it?'

'But they're going to execute her!'

'Better her than me.'

'I've seen her,' Luke persisted desperately. 'She's beautiful.'

'So's life.'

'She's a rich and powerful Senator,' Luke pressed, hoping an appeal to Solo's baser instincts might be more effective. 'If we could save her, the reward could be substantial.'

'Uh . . . rich?' Then Solo looked disdainful. 'Wait a minute . . . Reward, from whom? From the government on Alderaan?' He made a sweeping gesture towards the space where Alderaan had once orbited.

Luke thought furiously. 'If she's being held here and is scheduled to be executed, she must be dangerous to whoever destroyed Alderaan, to whoever had this station built. You can bet it had something to do with the Empire instituting a reign of full repression.

'I'll tell you who'll pay for her rescue, and for the information she holds. The Senate, the Rebel Alliance, and every concern that did business with Alderaan. She could be the sole surviving heir of the off-world wealth of the entire system! The reward could be more wealth than you can imagine.'

Solo glanced at Chewbacca, who grunted a terse reply. 'All right, we'll give it a try. But you'd better be right about that reward. What's your plan, kid?'

Luke was momentarily taken aback. He had no idea how to proceed. He had grown used to old Ben and Solo giving directions. Now the next move was up to him.

His eyes were caught by several metal circlets dangling from the belt of Solo's armour. 'Give me those binders and tell Chewbacca to come over here.'

Solo handed Luke the thin but quite unbreakable cuffs and relayed the request to Chewbacca. The Wookiee lumbered over and stood waiting next to Luke.

'Now, I'm going to put these on you,' Luke began, starting to move behind the Wookiee with the cuffs, 'and –'

Chewbacca made a sound low in his throat.

Solo sounded amused. 'Don't worry, Chewie. I think I know what he has in mind.'

The cuffs barely fit around the thick wrists. Despite his partner's seeming confidence in the plan, the Wookiee wore a worried, frightened look as the restraints were activated.

'Luke, sir.' Luke looked over at Threepio. 'Pardon me for asking, but, ah – what should Artoo and I do if someone discovers us here in your absence?'

'Hope they don't have blasters,' Solo replied.

Solo and Luke were too engrossed in their coming expedition to pay much attention to the worried robot.

They adjusted their helmets. Then, with Chewbacca wearing a downcast expression, they started along the corridor where Ben Kenobi had disappeared.

NINE

As they travelled farther and deeper into the bowels of the gigantic station, they found it increasingly difficult to maintain an air of casual indifference. Chewbacca also made it impossible for the two young men to be as inconspicuous as they would have liked.

The farther they travelled, the heavier the traffic became. Other soldiers, bureaucrats, technicians, and mechanicals bustled around them. Intent on their own assignments, they ignored the trio completely.

Eventually they reached a wide bank of elevators. Luke breathed a sigh of relief. The computer-controlled transport ought to be capable of taking them just about anywhere on the station in response to a verbal command.

Luke studied the operating panel, then tried to sound knowledgeable as he spoke into the pickup grid. The door slid shut and they were on their way. After what felt like hours, the door opened and they stepped out into the security area.

It had been Luke's hope they would discover something like the old-fashioned barred cells of the kind used on Tatooine in towns like Mos Eisley. Instead, they saw only narrow ramps bordering a bottomless ventilation shaft. These walkways, several levels of them, ran parallel to smooth curving walls which held faceless detention cells. Alert-looking guards and energy gates seemed to be everywhere they looked.

Uncomfortably aware that the longer they stood frozen in place, the sooner someone was bound to come over and ask unanswerable questions, Luke searched frantically for a course of action.

Luke's worst fears were realised. A tall, grim-looking officer approached them. He frowned as he examined the silent Chewbacca.

'Where are you two going with this – thing?'

A panicky Luke found himself replying almost instinctively. 'Prisoner transfer from block TS-138.'

The officer looked puzzled. 'I wasn't notified. I'll have to clear it.'

Turning, the man walked to a small console nearby and began entering his request.

Solo nodded to Luke as he unfastened Chewbacca's cuffs. Then he whispered something to the Wookiee. An ear-splitting howl shook the corridor as Chewbacca threw up both hands, grabbing Solo's rifle from him.

'Look out!' a seemingly terrified Solo shouted. 'It's loose. It'll rip us all apart!'

Both he and Luke had darted clear of the rampaging Wookiee, pulled out their pistols, and were blasting away at him. Not a single shot came close to the dodging Wookiee. Instead, they blasted automatic cameras, energy-rate controls, and the three dumbfounded guards.

The officer in charge was preparing to jab the general alarm when a burst from Luke's pistol caught him in the midsection and he fell without a word.

Solo rushed to the open comlink speaker, which was screeching anxious questions about what was going on.

Ignoring the barrage of alternate threats and queries, he checked the readout set in the panel nearby. 'We've got to find out which cell this Princess of yours is in. There must be a dozen levels and – Here it is. Cell 2187. Go on – Chewie and I'll hold them here.'

Luke nodded once and was racing down the narrow walkway.

After gesturing for the Wookiee to take up a position where he could cover the elevators, Solo took a deep breath and responded to the unceasing calls from the comlink.

'Everything's under control,' he said into the pickup, sounding official. 'Situation normal.'

'It didn't sound like that,' a voice snapped back in a no-nonsense tone. 'We're sending a squad up.'

'Negative – negative. We have an energy leak. Give us a few minutes to lock it down. Large leak – very dangerous.'

'Energy leak . . . Who is this? What's your operating – ?'

Pointing his pistol at the panels, Solo blew the instrumentation to silent scraps. Turning, he shouted down the corridor, 'Hurry it up, Luke! We're going to have company.'

Luke was absorbed in running from one cell to the next and studying the numbers glowing above each doorway. He found 2187 just as he was about to give up and try the next level down.

Turning his pistol to maximum, he opened fire on the door. When the weapon became too hot to hold, he tossed it from hand to hand. As he did so the smoke had time to clear, and he saw that the door had been blown away.

Peering through the smoke with an uncomprehending look on her face was the young woman whose portrait Artoo Detoo had projected on Tatooine.

She was even more beautiful than her image, Luke decided, staring dazedly at her. 'You're even – more beautiful – than I – '

Her look of confusion was replaced by impatience. 'Aren't you a little short for a storm trooper?' she finally commented.

'What? Oh – the uniform.' He removed the helmet. 'I've come to rescue you. I'm Luke Skywalker. Ben Kenobi is with me. We've got your two 'droids – '

The uncertainty was instantly replaced by hope. 'Ben Kenobi!' She looked around Luke, ignoring him as she searched for the Jedi. 'Where is he? Obi-wan!'

'He is here,' Vader stated unemotionally.

Tarkin looked startled. 'Obi-wan Kenobi! That's impossible. What makes you think so?'

'A stirring in the force, of a kind I've felt only in the presence of my old master. It is unmistakable.'

'Surely – surely he must be dead by now.'

Vader hesitated. 'Perhaps . . . It is gone now. It was only a brief sensation.'

'The Jedi are extinct,' declared Tarkin positively. 'Their fire was quenched decades ago. You, my friend, are all that's left of their ways.'

A comlink buzzed softly for attention. 'Yes?' Tarkin acknowledged.

'We have an emergency alert in detention block AA-23.'

'The Princess!' Tarkin yelped, jumping to his feet. Vader whirled, trying to stare through the walls.

'I knew it – Obi-wan *is* here. I knew I could not mistake a stirring in the force of such power.'

'Put all sections on alert,' Tarkin ordered through the comlink. Then he turned to stare at Vader. 'If you're right, he must not be allowed to escape.'

'Escape may not be Obi-wan Kenobi's intention,' Vader replied. 'He is the last of the Jedi – and the greatest. The danger he presents to us must not be underestimated – yet only I can deal with him.' His head snapped around to stare fixedly at Tarkin. 'Alone.'

Luke and Leia had started back up the corridor when a series of blinding explosions ripped the walkway ahead of them. Several troopers had tried coming through the elevator, only to be crisped one after another by Chewbacca. Disdaining the elevators, they had blasted a gaping hole through a wall. The opening was too large for Solo and the Wookiee to cover completely. In twos and threes, the Imperials were working their way into the detention block.

Retreating down the walkway, Han and Chewbacca encountered Luke and the Princess. 'We can't go back that way!' Solo told them.

'No, it looks like you've managed to cut off our only escape route,' Leia agreed readily. 'This is a detention area, you know. They don't build them with multiple exits.'

Breathing heavily, Solo turned to look her up and down. 'Begging your forgiveness, Your Highness,' he said sarcastically, 'but maybe you'd prefer it back in your cell?'

'There's got to be another way out,' Luke muttered, pulling a small transmitter unit from his belt and carefully adjusting the frequency: *'See Threepio . . . See Threepio!'*

A familiar voice responded with gratifying speed. 'Yes, sir?'

'We've been cut off here. Are there *any* other ways out of the detention area?'

Static crackled over the tiny grid as Solo and Chewbacca kept the Imperial troops bottled up at the other end of the walkway.

'What was that . . . ? I didn't copy.'

Back in the gantry office Artoo Detoo beeped and whistled frantically as Threepio adjusted controls, fighting to clear the awkward transmission. 'I said, all systems have been alerted to your presence, sir. The main entry seems to be the only way in or out of the cell block.'

Someone began banging on the locked door to the office – evenly at first and then more insistently.

'Oh, no!' Threepio groaned.

The smoke in the cell corridor was now so intense that it was difficult for Solo and Chewbacca to pick their targets.

Every so often one of the soldiers would attempt to move closer, only to stand exposed as he penetrated the smoke. Under the accurate fire of the two smugglers, he would rapidly join the accumulating mass of motionless figures on the rampway flooring.

Energy bolts continued to ricochet wildly through the block as Luke moved close to Solo.

'There isn't any other way out,' he yelled over the deafening roar of concentrated fire.

'Well, they're closing in on us. What do we do now?'

'This is some rescue,' an irritated voice complained from behind them. Both men turned to see a thoroughly disgusted Princess eyeing them with regal disapproval. 'When you came in here, didn't you have a plan for getting out?'

Solo nodded towards Luke. 'He's the brains, sweetheart.'

Luke managed an embarrassed grin and shrugged helplessly. He turned to help return fire, but before he could do so, the Princess had snatched the pistol from his hand.

'Hey!'

Luke stared as she moved along the wall, finally locating a small grate nearby. She pointed the pistol at it and fired.

Solo gazed at her in disbelief. 'What do you think you're doing?'

'It looks like it's up to me to save our skins. Get into that garbage chute, flyboy!'

While the others looked on in amazement, she jumped feet first into the opening and disappeared.

Shoving the reluctant Wookiee towards the tiny opening, Solo helped jam the massive bulk through. As soon as he disappeared, the Corellian followed him in. Luke fired off a last series of blasts, slid into the chute, and was gone.

The chamber Luke tumbled into was dimly lit. Unadorned except for the concealed illuminants, the garbage room was at least a quarter full of slimy muck, much of which had already achieved a state of decomposition.

Solo was stumbling around the edge of the room,

slipping and sinking up to his knees in the uncertain footing in an attempt to locate an exit. All he found was a small, thick hatchway which he grunted and heaved to pry open. The hatchcover refused to budge.

'The garbage chute was a wonderful idea,' he told the Princess sardonically, wiping the sweat from his forehead. 'Unfortunately, we can't ride out of here on a drifting odour, and there doesn't seem to be any other exit. Unless I can get this hatch open.'

Stepping back, he pulled his pistol and fired at the cover. The bolt promptly went howling around the room as everyone sought cover in the garbage. A last glance and the bolt detonated almost on top of them.

Looking less dignified by the moment, Leia was the first to emerge from the pungent cover. 'Put that thing away,' she told Solo grimly, 'or you're going to get us all killed.'

'Yes, Your Worship,' Solo muttered. He made no move to reholster his weapon.

'We had things well under control – until you led us down here.'

'Sure you did,' she shot back, brushing refuse from her hair and shoulders. 'Oh, well, it could be worse . . . '

A piercing, horrible moaning filled the room. It seemed to come from somewhere beneath them. Chewbacca let out a terrified yowl of his own and tried to flatten himself against a wall. Luke drew his pistol and peered hard at various clumps of debris.

'What was that?' Solo asked.

'I'm not too sure.' With shocking suddenness Luke disappeared straight down into the garbage.

'It's got Luke!' the Princess shouted. 'It took him under!' Solo looked around frantically for something to shoot at.

As abruptly as he had vanished, Luke reappeared. A thick whitish tentacle was wrapped tight around his throat.

'Shoot it, kill it!' Luke screamed.

Once again Luke was sucked under. Solo stared helplessly around the multicoloured surface.

There was a distant rumble of heavy machinery, and two opposing walls of the chamber moved inward several centimetres. The rumble ceased and then it was quiet again. Luke appeared close to Solo, scrabbling his way clear of the suffocating mess and rubbing at the welt on his neck.

'What happened to it?' Leia wondered, eyeing the garbage warily.

Luke looked puzzled. 'I don't know. It just let me go and disappeared.'

'I've got a very bad feeling about this,' Solo murmured.

Again the distant rumble filled the room; again the walls began their inward march. Only this time neither sound nor movement showed any sign of stopping.

'Don't just stand there gaping at each other!' the Princess urged them. 'Try to brace them with something.'

Even with the thick poles and old metal beams Chewbacca could handle, they were unable to find anything capable of slowing the walls' advance.

Luke pulled out his comlink. 'Threepio . . . come in, Threepio!' A decent pause produced no response.

He tried again. 'See Threepio, come in. Do you read?'

'Help, help! Let us out!'

Several of the troopers opened the noisy cabinet. Two robots, one tall and humanoid, the other purely mechanical and three-legged, stepped out into the office. The taller one gave the impression of being half unbalanced with fear.

'They're madmen, I tell you, madmen!' He gestured urgently towards the doorway. 'I think they said something about heading for the prison level. They just left. If you hurry, you might catch them. That way, that way!'

Two of the troopers inside joined those waiting in the hallway in hustling off down the corridor. That left two guards to watch over the office. They totally ignored the robots as they discussed what might have taken place.

'All the excitement has overloaded the circuitry in my companion here,' Threepio explained carefully. 'If you don't mind, I'd like to take him down to Maintenance.'

'Hmmm?' One of the guards looked up indifferently and nodded to the robot. Threepio and Artoo hurried out the door without looking back. As they departed it occurred to the guard that the taller of the two 'droids was of a type he had never seen before. He shrugged. That was not surprising on a station of this size.

'That was too close,' Threepio muttered as they scurried down an empty corridor. 'Now we'll have to find another information-control console and plug you back in, or everything is lost.'

The garbage chamber grew remorselessly smaller, the smoothly fitting metal walls moving towards one another with stolid precision. Larger pieces of refuse performed a concerto of snapping and popping that was rising towards a final shuddering crescendo.

Chewbacca whined pitifully as he fought with all his incredible strength and weight to hold back one of the walls.

Luke paused for breath, shaking the innocent comlink angrily. 'What could have happened to Threepio?'

'Try the hatch again,' advised Liea. 'It's our only hope.'

Solo shielded his eyes and did so. The ineffectual blast echoed mockingly through the narrowing chamber.

The service bay was unoccupied. After a cautious survey, Threepio beckoned for Artoo to follow. Together they commenced a hurried search of the many service panels. Artoo let out a beep, and Threepio rushed to him. He waited impatiently as the smaller unit plugged the receptive arm carefully into the open socket.

Less than a metre of life was left to the trapped occupants of the garbage room. Leia and Solo had been forced to turn sideways, facing each other. The haughtiness was gone from the Princess's face. Reaching out, she took Solo's hand, clutching it convulsively as she felt the first touch of the closing walls.

Luke had fallen and was lying on his side, fighting to keep his head above the rising ooze. He nearly choked on a mouthful of compressed sludge when his comlink began buzzing for attention.

'Threepio!'

'Are you there, sir?' the 'droid replied. 'We've had some minor problems. You would not believe – '

'Shut up, Threepio!' Luke screamed into the unit. 'And shut down all the refuse units on the detention level or immediately below it. Do you copy? Shut down the refuse – '

Moments later Threepio grabbed at his head in pain as a terrific screeching and yelling sounded over the comlink.

In fact, they were shouts of relief. The chamber walls had reversed direction automatically with Artoo's shutdown and were moving apart again.

'Artoo, Threepio,' Luke hollered into the comlink, 'it's all right, we're all right! Do you read me? We're O.K. – you did just fine.'

Brushing at the clinging slime, he made his way as rapidly as possible towards the hatchcover. Bending, he scraped accumulated detritus away, noting the number thus revealed.

'Open the pressure-maintenance hatch on unit 366-117891.'

'Yes, sir,' came Threepio's acknowledgement.

TEN

Lined with power cables and circuitry conduits that rose from the depths and vanished into the heavens, the service trench appeared to be hundreds of kilometres deep. The narrow catwalk running around one side looked like a starched thread glued on a glowing ocean. It was barely wide enough for one man to traverse.

One man edged his way along that treacherous walkway now, his gaze intent on something ahead of him. The clacking sounds of enormous switching devices resounded in the vast open space.

Two thick cables joined beneath an overlay panel. It was locked, but after careful inspection of sides, top and bottom, Ben Kenobi pressed the panel cover, causing it to spring aside. A blinking computer terminal was revealed beneath.

With care he performed adjustments to the terminal. Several indicator lights on the board changed from red to blue.

Without warning, a door behind him opened. Hurriedly reclosing the panel cover, the old man slipped deeper into the shadows. A detachment of troopers had appeared, and the officer in charge moved within a couple of metres of the motionless, hidden figure.

'Secure this area until the alert has been cancelled.'

As they began to disperse, Kenobi became one with the dark.

The hallway they had emerged into gave the impression of not having been used since the station had been built. He had no idea where they were.

Something hit the wall behind them with a massive *thunk*, and Luke yelled for everyone to watch out as a long, gelatinous limb worked its way through the hatch and flailed hopefully about in the open corridor. Solo aimed his pistol at it.

'No, wait! It'll be heard!' Leia shouted.

Solo ignored her and fired at the hatchway. The burst of energy was rewarded with a distant roar as an avalanche of weakened wall all but buried the creature in the chamber beyond.

Magnified by the narrow corridor, the sounds continued to roll and echo for long minutes afterwards. Luke shook his head in disgust. Until now he had looked up to the Corellian. But the senseless gesture of firing at the hatchway brought them, in Luke's mind, to the same level.

The Princess's actions were more surprising than Solo's, however. 'Listen,' she began, 'I don't know where you came from, but I'm grateful. But from now on you do as I tell you.'

Solo gaped at her. 'Look, Your Holiness, I take orders only from one person – me.'

'It's a wonder you're still alive,' she shot back. A quick look down the corridor and she started determinedly off in the other direction.

Solo looked at Luke, and shook his head. 'No reward is worth putting up with *her* . . . Hey, slow down!'

Leia had started around a bend in the corridor, and they ran swiftly to catch up with her.

The half dozen troops milling around the entrance to the power trench were so interested in discussing the peculiar disturbance in the detention block that they failed to notice the fey wraith behind them. It moved from shadow to shadow like a night-stalking ferret, freezing when one of the troopers seemed to turn slightly in its direction, moving on again as if walking on air.

Several minutes later one of the troopers frowned, turning to where he thought he had sensed a movement near the opening to the main passageway. There was nothing but an undefinable something which the ghost-like Kenobi had left behind. Acutely uncomfortable yet unwilling to confess to hallucinations, the trooper turned back to the more prosaic conversation of his fellows.

Someone finally discovered the two unconscious guards tied in the service lockers on board the captured freighter.

Troopers carried their two armourless comrades down the ramp and towards the nearest hospital bay. On the way they passed two forms hidden by a small opened service panel. Threepio and Artoo went unnoticed.

As soon as the troops had passed they hunted for the proper outlet.

Luke, Solo, Chewbacca, and the Princess reached the end of an empty hallway. It dead-ended before a large window which overlooked a hangar, giving them a sweeping view of the freighter below.

Pulling out his comlink, Luke spoke into the pickup. 'See Threepio . . . do you copy?'

There was a threatening pause, then, 'I read you, sir. We had to abandon the region around the office.'

'Are you both safe?'

'For the moment. We're in the main hangar, across from the ship.'

Luke looked towards the bay window. 'I can't see you – we must be right above you. Stand by. We'll join you as soon as we can.'

'Wonder if the old man was able to knock out the tractor,' Solo was muttering as he surveyed the scene below. A dozen or so troopers were moving in and out of the freighter.

Leia Organa turned to glance in surprise from the ship to Solo. 'You came here in that wreck? You're braver than I thought.'

Rounding a corner, the three humans came to an abrupt halt. So did the twenty Imperial troopers march-

111

ing towards them. Reacting naturally. Solo drew his pistol and charged the platoon, yelling and howling in several languages at the top of his lungs.

Startled by the unexpected assault and wrongly assuming their attacker knew what he was doing, the troopers started to back away. Several wild shots from the Corellian's pistol initiated complete panic. Ranks and composure shattered, the troopers broke and fled down the passage.

Drunk with his own prowess, Solo continued the chase, turning to shout back at Luke, 'Get to the ship. I'll take care of these!' Chewbacca let out a thunderous howl and rushed down the hallway after him.

'That's done it,' Luke growled disgustedly. 'Let's go.' Together they started off in search of a way down to a hangar-deck level.

Solo continued his rout of all opposition, running at top speed down the long hallway, yelling and brandishing his pistol.

Half the troops had already scattered down various sub-passages and corridors. The ten troopers he continued to harry raced headlong away from him, returning his fire only indifferently. Then they came up against a dead end, which forced them to turn and confront their opponents. Solo and Imperials regarded one another silently. Several of the troopers were staring, not at him but past him.

It suddenly occurred to Solo that he was alone, and the same thought was beginning to seep into the minds of the guards. Rifles and pistols started to come up. Solo took a step backwards, fired one shot, then turned and ran.

Chewbacca was debating what to do when Solo came tearing around a corner and nearly ran him down. Seeing ten troopers in pursuit, the Wookiee turned and followed Solo back up the hallway.

Luke grabbed the Princess and pulled her back into a

recess. A squad of soldiers hurried past, responding to the alarms that continued to ring steadily. Luke looked out at the retreating backs and tried to catch his breath. 'Our only hope of reaching the ship is from the other side of the hangar. They already know someone's here.' He started back down the corridor, motioning for her to follow.

Two guards appeared at the far end of the passageway, paused, and pointed directly at them. Turning, Luke and Leia began running back the way they had come. A larger squad of troopers rounded the far bend and came racing towards them.

Blocked ahead and behind, they hunted frantically for another way out. Then Leia spotted the cramped subhallway and gestured to it.

Luke fired at the nearest of their pursuers and joined her in running down the narrow passage. It looked like a minor service corridor. Behind them, pursuit sounded deafening in the confining space. But it minimised the amount of fire the troops could concentrate on them.

A thick hatchway appeared ahead. The lighting beyond turned dimmer, raising Luke's hopes. If they could lock the hatch even for a few moments and lose themselves beyond, they might have a chance of shaking their tormentors.

But the hatch stayed open, showing no inclination to close automatically. Luke was about to let out a shout when the ground suddenly vanished ahead of him. His toes hanging over nothingness, he flailed to regain his balance.

The catwalk had been reduced to a stub protruding into empty air. Luke studied walls that soared to unseen heights overhead and plunged to fathomless depths below. The service shaft was employed in circulating and recycling the atmosphere of the station.

Other dangers competed for Luke's attention. A burst of energy exploded above their heads, sending metal slivers flying.

'I think we made a wrong turn,' he murmured, firing back at the advancing troops.

An open hatchway showed on the other side of the chasm. It might as well have been a light-year away. Hunting along the rim of the doorway, Leia located a switch and hit it quickly. The hatch door behind them slid shut with a resounding boom. That cut off fire from the rapidly nearing soldiers, but it also left the two fugitives balanced precariously on a small section of catwalk barely a metre square.

Gesturing for the Princess to move aside, Luke aimed the pistol at the hatch controls. A brief burst of energy melted them flush with the wall, insuring that no one could open it easily from the other side. Then he turned his attention to the vast cavity blocking their path to the opposite portal – a small yellow rectangle of freedom.

'We've got to get across there somehow,' Leia said, examining the metal bordering the sealed doorway. 'Find the controls for extending the bridge.'

Some desperate searching produced nothing, while an ominous pounding and hissing sounded from behind the frozen door. A small spot of white appeared in the centre of the metal, then began to spread and smoke.

'They're coming through!' Luke groaned.

The Princess turned carefully to stare across the gap. 'This must be a single-unit bridge, with the controls only on the other side.'

Reaching up to the point at the panel holding the unreachable controls, Luke's hand caught on something at his wrist. The cable coiled tightly in small loops was thin and fragile seeming, but it would hold Leia and himself. Pulling the cable free of the waist catch, he gauged its length, matching it against the width of the abyss.

Luke removed a small but heavy power unit from the utility belt of his armour and tied one end of the cable around it. Making sure the wrapping was secure, he stepped as close to the edge of their uncertain perch as he dared.

Whirling the weighted end of the cord in increasing circles, he let it arc across the gorge. It struck an out-cropping of cylindrical conduits on the other side and fell downward. He pulled the loose line back in, then recoiled it for another try.

Once again the weighted end orbited in ever greater circles, and again he flung it across the gap. He could feel the rising heat behind him from the melting metal doorway.

This time the heavy end looped around an outcrop-ping of pipes above, wrapped itself several times around, and slipped, battery end down, into a crack between them. Leaning backwards, he tugged and pulled on the cable. The cable showed no sign of parting.

Wrapping the other end of the line several times around his waist and right arm, he reached out and pulled the Princess close to him with the other. The hatch door behind them was now a molten white, and liquid metal was running steadily from its borders.

Something warm and pleasant touched Luke's lips. He looked down in shock at the Princess, his mouth still tingling from the kiss.

'Just for luck,' she murmured with a slight, almost embarrassed smile. 'We're going to need it.'

Gripping the thin cable as tightly as possible with his left hand, Luke put his right over it, took a deep breath, and jumped out into air.

In a moment Luke was on the other side, scrambling on his knees to make sure they didn't fall back into the pit. Leia released her hold on him, rolled forward and into the open hatchway, climbing to her feet as Luke fought to untangle himself from the cable.

A distant whine became a loud hiss, then a groan as the hatch door on the other side gave way. It collapsed inwards and tumbled into the depths.

A few bolts struck the wall nearby. Luke turned his own weapon on the unsuccessful troopers and returned the fire even as Leia was pulling him into the passage-way behind.

Once clear of the door he hit the activating switch. It shut tightly behind them. They would have several minutes, without having to worry about being shot. On the other hand, Luke didn't have the slightest idea where they were.

Solo and his Wookiee partner had succeeded in shaking a portion of their pursuers. But it seemed that whenever they slipped free of several soldiers, more appeared to take their place.

Ahead, a series of shield doors was beginning to close. 'Hurry, Chewie!' Solo urged.

Despite his immense strength, the Wookiee was not built for long-distance sprinting. Only his enormous stride had enabled him to keep pace with the lithe Corellian. Both slipped inside one of the doors just before the five layers slammed shut.

Kenobi had avoided one patrol after another, slowly working his way back towards the docking bay holding the freighter. Just another two turns and he should be at the hangar. What he would do then would be determined by how inconspicuous his charges had been.

Ben sensed something directly ahead and slowed cautiously. It had a familiar feel to it, a half-remembered mental odour he could not quite place.

Then the figure stepped out in front of him, blocking his entry to the hangar not five metres away. The outline and size of the figure completed the puzzle. His hand moved naturally to the hilt of his deactivated sabre.

'I have been waiting a long time, Obiwan Kenobi,' Darth Vader intoned solemnly. 'We meet again at last. The circle has been completed.' Kenobi sensed satisfaction beneath the hideous mask. 'The presence I sensed earlier could only have been you.'

Kenobi regarded the great form blocking his retreat and nodded slowly. 'You still have much to learn.'

'You were once my teacher,' Vader admitted, 'and I learned much from you. But the time of learning has

116

long passed, and I am the master now.'

There would be no reasoning here, Kenobi knew. Igniting his sabre, he assumed the pose of warrior-ready, a movement accomplished with the ease and elegance of a dancer.

Rather roughly, Vader imitated the movement. Several minutes followed without motion as the two men remained staring at each other, as if waiting for some unspoken signal.

Kenobi blinked once, shook his head, and tried to clear his eyes, which had begun to water slightly. Sweat beaded up on his forehead, and his eyelids fluttered again.

'Your powers are weak,' Vader noted emotionlessly. 'Old man, you should never have come back.'

'You sense only a part of the force, Darth,' Kenobi murmured. 'As always, you perceive its reality as little as a utensil perceives the taste of food.'

Executing a move of incredible swiftness for one so old, Kenobi lunged at the massive shape. Vader blocked the stab with equal speed, riposting with a counterslash that Kenobi barely parried. Another parry and Kenobi countered again using this opportunity to move around the towering Dark Lord.

They continued to trade blows, with the old man now backing towards the hangar. Once, his sabre and Vader's locked, the interaction of the two energy fields producing a violent sparking and flashing. A low buzzing sound rose from the straining power units as each sabre sought to override the other.

Threepio peeked around the entrance to the docking bay, worriedly counting the number of troopers milling around the deserted freighter.

He ducked back out of sight just as one of the guards glanced in his direction. A second, more cautious appraisal was more rewarding. It revealed Han Solo and Chewbacca hugging the wall of another tunnel on the far side of the bay.

Solo also was nonplussed at the number of guards. He muttered, 'Didn't we just leave this party?'

Chewbacca grunted, and both turned, only to relax and lower their weapons at the sight of Luke and the Princess.

'What kept you?' Solo quipped.

'We ran into,' Leia explained, panting heavily, 'some old friends.'

Luke was staring at the freighter. 'Is the ship all right?'

'Seems O.K.,' was Solo's analysis. 'It doesn't look like they've removed anything or disturbed her engines. The problem's going to be getting to it.'

Leia suddenly pointed to one of the opposite tunnels. 'Look!'

Illuminated by the flare from contacting energy fields, Ben Kenobi and Darth Vader were backing towards the bay. The fight attracted the attention of others besides the Senator. Every one of the guards moved in for a better view of the Olympian conflict.

'Now's our chance,' Solo observed, starting forward.

All seven of the troopers guarding the ship broke and rushed towards the combatants, going to the Dark Lord's aid. Threepio barely ducked aside as they ran past him. Turning back into the alcove, he yelled to his companion.

'Unplug yourself, Artoo. We're leaving.' As soon as the Artoo unit slipped his sensor arm free of the socket, the two 'droids began to slowly edge out into the open bay.

Kenobi heard the approaching commotion and spared a glance back into the hangar. The squad of troopers bearing down on him was enough to show that he was trapped.

Vader took immediate advantage of the momentary distraction to bring his sabre over and down. Kenobi somehow managed to deflect the sweeping blow, at once parrying and turning a complete circle.

'You still have your skill, but your power fades. Prepare to meet the force, Obi-wan.'

Kenobi gauged the shrinking distance between the oncoming troops and himself, then turned a pitying gaze on Vader. 'This is a fight you cannot win, Darth. Your power has matured since I taught you, but I too have grown much since our parting. If my blade finds its mark, you will cease to exist. But if you cut me down, I will only become more powerful. Heed my words.'

'Your philosophies no longer confuse me, old man,' Vader growled contemptuously. 'I am the master now.'

Once again he lunged forward, feinting, and then slashing in a deadly downward arc with the sabre. It struck home, cutting the old man cleanly in half. There was a brief flash as Kenobi's cloak fluttered to the deck in two neat sections.

But Ben Kenobi was not in it. Vader poked at the empty cloak sections with the sabre. There was no sign of the old man. He had vanished as though he had never existed.

The guards slowed their approach and joined Vader in examining the place where Kenobi had stood seconds before. Several of them muttered, and even the awesome presence of the Sith Lord couldn't keep a few of them from feeling a little afraid.

Once the guards had turned and dashed for the far tunnel, Solo and the others started for the starship – until Luke saw Kenobi cut in two. Instantly he shifted direction and was moving towards the guards.

'Ben!' he screamed, firing wildly towards the troops. Solo cursed, but turned to fire in support of Luke.

One of the energy bolts struck the safety release on the tunnel blast door. The emergency hold broken, the heavy door fairly exploded downward. Both the guards and Vader leaped clear – the guards into the bay and Vader backwards, to the opposite side of the door.

Solo had turned and started for the entrance to the

119

ship, but he paused as he saw Luke running towards the guards.

'It's too late!' Leia yelled at him. 'It's over.'

'No!' Luke half shouted, half sobbed.

A familiar, yet different voice rang in his ears – Ben's voice. 'Luke . . . listen!' was all it said.

Bewildered, Luke turned to hunt for the source of that admonition. He only saw Leia beckoning to him as she followed Artoo and Threepio up the ramp.

'Come on! There's no time.'

Hesitating, his mind still on that imagined voice, a confused Luke took aim and felled several soldiers before he, too, whirled and retreated into the freighter.

ELEVEN

Dazed, Luke staggered towards the front of the ship. He barely noticed the sound of energy bolts exploding harmlessly outside. With misty eyes he stared as Chewbacca and Solo adjusted controls.

Leia Organa removed her cloak. Moving to him, she placed it gently around his shoulders.

'There wasn't anything you could have done,' she whispered comfortingly. 'It was all over in an instant.'

'I can't believe he's gone,' came Luke's reply, his voice a ghost of a whisper. 'I can't.'

Solo shifted a lever, staring nervously ahead. But the massive bay door was constructed to respond to the approach of any vessel. The freighter slipped quickly past the still-opening door and out into free space.

Whirling, Solo ran out of the cockpit. 'Come with me, kid,' he shouted at Luke. 'We're not out of this yet.'

Leia turned an angry face to Solo. 'Leave him alone. Can't you see what the old man meant to him?'

'So what?' The old man gave himself to give us a chance to get away. You want to waste that, Luke?'

Without a word, Luke threw off the cloak and joined Solo.

Giving him a reassuring smile, Solo gestured down a narrow accessway. Luke smiled grimly, and rushed down it as Solo started down the opposing passage.

Luke found himself in a large rotating bubble protruding from the side of the ship. He settled himself into the seat and commenced a rapid study of the controls. Activator here, firing grip here . . . He had fired such weapons a thousand times before – in his dreams.

The starfield wheeled around Luke as an Imperial Tie fighter raced towards him and then swung overhead to vanish into the distance. Within the tiny cockpit its pilot frowned as the battered freighter darted out of range. Adjusting his controls, he swung up and over in a high arc intended to take him on a fresh intercept course with the escaping ship.

Solo fired at another fighter, and its pilot nearly slammed his engine through its mountings as he fought to avoid the powerful energy bolts. As he did so, his hurried manoeuvre brought him under and around to the other side of the freighter. Even as he was lowering the glare reflector over his eyes, Luke opened up on the racing fighter.

Chewbacca was alternating his attention between the instruments and the tracking screens, while Leia strained to separate distant stars from nearby assassins.

Two fighters dove simultaneously on the twisting, spiralling freighter, trying to line their weapons on the unexpectedly flexible craft. Solo fired at the descending globes, and Luke followed with his own weapon a second later. Both fired on the starship and then shot past.

'They're coming in too fast,' Luke yelled into his comlink.

Another enemy bolt struck the freighter forward and was barely shunted aside by its deflectors. The cockpit shuddered violently, and gauges whined in protest at the quantity of energy they were being asked to monitor and compensate for.

Chewbacca muttered something to Leia, and she murmured a soft reply as if she almost understood.

Another fighter unloosed a barrage on the freighter. This time the bolt pierced an overloaded screen and actually struck the side of the ship. Though partially deflected, it still carried enough power to blow out a large control panel in the main passageway, sending a rain of sparks and smoke in all directions. Artoo Detoo started stolidly toward the miniature inferno as the ship lurched crazily, throwing the less stable Threepio into a cabinet full of component chips.

Then a fighter floated down on the damaged freighter, right into Luke's sights. Luke fired at it. The agile little vessel darted out of his range, but as it passed beneath them Solo picked it up instantly, and commenced a steady following fire. The fighter erupted in an incredible flash of multicoloured light.

Solo whirled and gave Luke a victory wave, which the younger man gleefully returned. Then they turned back to their weapons as yet another fighter stormed over the freighter's hull, firing at its transmitter dish.

In the middle of the main passageway, angry flames raged around a stubby cylindrical shape. A fine white powdery spray issued from Artoo Detoo's head. Wherever it touched, the fire retreated sharply.

Luke tried to relax, to become a part of the weapon. Almost without being aware of it, he was firing at a retreating Imperial. When he blinked, it was to see the flaming fragments of the enemy craft forming a perfect ball of light outside the turret. It was his turn to spin and flash the Corellian a grin of triumph.

In the cockpit, Leia paid close attention to scattered readouts as well as searching the sky for additional ships. She directed her voice towards an open mike.

'There are still two more out there. Looks like we've

lost the lateral monitors and the starboard deflector shield.'

'Don't worry,' Solo told her, 'she'll hold together.'

A Tie fighter seemed to materialise out of nowhere, energy bolts reaching out from it towards him. Its companion craft came up on the freighter's other side and Luke found himself firing steadily at it. At the last possible instant before it passed out of range, he swung the weapon's nozzle minutely, his finger tightening convulsively on the fire control. The Imperial fighter turned into a rapidly expanding cloud of phosphorescing dust. The other fighter retreated at top speed.

'We've made it!' Leia shouted, turning to give the startled Wookiee an unexpected hug. He growled at her – very slowly.

Darth Vader strode into the control room where Governor Tarkin stood staring at a huge, brilliantly lit screen. He barely glanced around as Vader entered.

'Are they away?' the Dark Lord demanded.

'They've just completed the jump to hyperspace.' Tarkin turned to face Vader, a hint of warning in his tone.

'I'm taking an awful chance, on your insistence, Vader. Are you certain the homing beacon is secure aboard their ship?'

Vader exuded confidence beneath the reflective black mask. 'There is nothing to fear. This will be a day long remembered. It already has been witness to the final extinction of the Jedi. Soon it will see the end of the Alliance and the rebellion.'

Solo switched places with Chewbacca, the Wookiee grateful for the opportunity to relinquish the controls. As the Corellian moved aft to check the extent of the damage, a determined-looking Leia passed him in the corridor.

'The important thing is not my safety, but the fact

123

that the information in the R-2 'droid is still intact,' she admitted.

'What's that 'droid carrying that's so important?'

Leia considered the blazing starfield forward. 'Complete technical schematics of the battle station. I only hope that when the data is analysed, a weakness can be found. Until the station itself is destroyed, we must go on. This war isn't over yet.'

'It is for me,' objected the pilot. 'I'm not on this mission for your revolution. Economics interest me, not politics. There's business to be done under any government. I expect to be well paid for risking my ship and my hide.'

'You needn't worry about your reward,' she assured him. 'If money is what you love . . . that's what you will receive.'

Yavin was not a habitable world. The huge gas giant was patterned with pastel high-altitude cloud formations. Here and there the softly lambent atmosphere was moulded by cyclonic storms composed of six-hundred-kilometre-per-hour winds which boiled rolling gases up from the Yavinesque troposphere. It was a world of lingering beauty and quick death for any who might try to penetrate to its comparatively small core of frozen liquids.

Several of the giant planet's numerous moons, however, were planet-sized themselves, and of these, three could support humanoid life. Particularly inviting was the satellite designated as number four. It shone like an emerald in Yavin's necklace of moons, rich with plant and animal life. But it was not listed among those worlds supporting human settlement. Yavin was located too far from the settled regions of the galaxy.

Perhaps the latter reason had been responsible for whatever race had once risen from satellite four's jungles, only to disappear long before the first human explorer set foot on the tiny world.

Now all that remained were the mounds and foliage-clad clumps formed by jungle-covered buildings. But though they had sunk back into the dust, their artifacts and their world continued to serve an important purpose.

Strange sounds surged continually from one particular place. Here lay the most impressive of those edifices which a vanished race had raised towards the heavens. It was a temple, a roughly pyramidal structure so colossal that it seemed impossible it could have been built without the aid of modern gravitonic construction techniques. Yet all evidence pointed only to simple machines, hand technology – and, perhaps, devices alien and long lost.

From these monstrous blocks of solid rock, the massive temple had been constructed. The jungle had scaled even its soaring crest, clothing it in rich green and brown. Only near its base, in the temple front, did the jungle slide away completely, to reveal a long, dark entrance cut by its builders and enlarged to suit the needs of the structure's present occupants.

A tiny machine, its smooth metal sides and silvery hue incongruous amidst the all-pervasive green, appeared in the forest. It hummed like a fat, swollen beetle as it conveyed its cluster of passengers towards the open temple base. Crossing a considerable clearing, it was soon swallowed up by the dark maw in the front of the massive structure, leaving the jungle once more in the paws and claws of invisible squallers and screechers.

The original builders would never have recognised the interior of their temple. Seamed metal had replaced rock, and poured panelling did service for chamber division in place of wood. Buried layers excavated into the rock below, contained hangar upon hangar linked by powerful elevators.

A landspeeder came to a gradual stop within the temple, whose first level was the uppermost of those ship-filled hangars. Its engine died obediently as the vehicle settled to the ground. A noisy cluster of humans waiting nearby ceased their conversation and rushed towards the craft.

Fortunately Leia Organa quickly emerged from the speeder, or the man who reached it first might have pulled her bodily from it, so great was his delight at the sight of her.

'You're safe! We'd feared you'd been killed.' Abruptly he composed himself, stepped away from her, and executed a formal bow. 'When we heard about Alderaan, we were afraid that you were . . . lost along with the rest of the population.'

'All that is past history, Commander Willard,' she said. 'We have a future to live for. Alderaan and its people are gone. We must see that such does not happen again.

'We don't have time for our sorrows, Commander,' she continued briskly. 'The battle station has surely tracked us here.'

Solo started to protest, but she shut him up with logic and a stern look.

'That's the only explanation for the ease of our escape. They sent only four Tie fighters after us. They could as easily have launched a hundred.'

Solo had no reply for that, but continued to fume silently. Then Leia gestured at Artoo Detoo.

'You must use the information locked in this R-2 'droid to form a plan of attack. It's our only hope. The station itself is more powerful than anyone suspected.' Her voice dropped. 'If the data does not yield a weakness, there will be no stopping them.'

Luke was then treated to a sight unique in his experience. Several rebel technicians walked up to Artoo Detoo, positioned themselves around him, and gently hoisted him in their arms. This was the first, and probably the last time he would ever see a robot being carried respectfully by men.

Theoretically, no weapon could penetrate the exceptionally dense stone of the ancient temple, but Luke

126

had seen the shattered remains of Alderaan and knew that for those in the incredible battle station the entire moon would present simply another abstract problem in mass-energy conversion.

Little Artoo Detoo rested comfortably in a place of honour, his body radiating computer and data-bank hookups like a metal hairdo. On an array of screens and readouts nearby the technical information stored on the submicroscopic record tape within the robot's brain was being played out. Hours of it – diagrams, charts, statistics.

First the rush of material was slowed and digested by more sophisticated computer minds. Then the most critical information was turned over to human analysts for detailed evaluation.

All the while See Threepio stood close to Artoo, marvelling at how so much complex data could be stored in the mind of so simple a 'droid.

The central briefing room was located deep within the bowels of the temple. The long, low-ceilinged auditorium was dominated by a raised dais and huge electronic display screen at its far end. Pilots, navigators, and a sprinkling of Artoo units filled the seats. Impatient, and feeling very out of place, Han Solo and Chebacca stood as far away from the stage as possible. Solo scanned the crowd, searching for Luke. The crazy kid had gone and joined the regular pilots. He didn't see Luke, but he recognised the Princess as she talked sombrely with some bemedalled oldster.

When a tall, dignified gentleman moved to stand by the far side of the screen, Solo turned his attention to him, as did everyone else in the room. General Jan Dodonna adjusted the tiny mike on his chest and indicated the small group seated close to him.

'You all know these people,' he intoned. 'They are the Senators and Generals whose worlds have given us support. They have come to be with us in what may well prove to be the decisive moment.

'The Imperial battle station you now all have heard of is approaching from the far side of Yavin and its sun. That gives us a little extra time, but it must be stopped – once and for all – before it can bring its weaponry to bear on us as it did on Alderaan.' A murmur ran through the crowd at the mention of that world, so callously obliterated.

'The station,' Dodonna went on, 'is heavily shielded and mounts more firepower than half the Imperial fleet. But its defences were designed to fend off large-scale, capital ship assaults. A small, one- or two-man fighter should be able to slip through its defensive screens.'

A slim, supple man rose. Dodonna acknowledged his presence. 'What is it, Red Leader?'

The man gestured towards the display screen, which showed a computer portrait of the battle station. 'Pardon me for asking, sir, but what good are our *snub* fighters going to be against *that*?'

Dodonna considered. 'Well, the Empire doesn't think a one-man fighter is any threat to anything except another small ship, like a Tie fighter, or they would have provided tighter screens. Apparently they're convinced that their defensive weaponry can fend off any light attacks.

'But an analysis of the plans provided by Princess Leia has revealed what we think is a weakness in the station's design. A big ship couldn't get near it, but an X- or Y-wing fighter might.

'It's a small thermal exhaust port. Its size belies its importance, as it appears to be an unshielded shaft that runs directly into the main reactor system powering the station. Since this serves as an emergency outlet for waste heat in the event of reactor over-production, its usefulness would be eliminated by particle shielding. A direct hit would initiate a chain reaction that will destroy the station.'

Mutterings of disbelief ran through the room.

'I didn't say your approach would be easy,' Dodonna admonished them. He gestured at the screen. 'You must manoeuvre straight in down this shaft, level off in the trench, and skim the surface to – this point. The target is only two metres across. It will take a precise hit at exactly ninety degrees to reach the reactor systematisation. And only a direct hit will start the complete reaction.

'I said the port wasn't particle-shielded. However, it is completely ray-shielded. That means no energy beams. You'll have to use proton torpedoes.'

A few of the pilots laughed humourlessly. One of them was a teenaged fighter jockey seated next to Luke who bore the unlikely name of Wedge Antilles. Artoo Detoo was there also, seated next to another Artoo unit who emitted a long whistle of hopelessness.

'A two-metre target at maximum speed – with a torpedo, yet,' Antilles snorted. 'That's impossible even for the computer.'

'But it's not impossible,' protested Luke. 'I used to bulls-eye womp-rats in my T-16 back home. They're not much bigger than two metres.'

'Is that so?' the rakishly uniformed youth noted derisively. 'Tell me, when you were going after your particular varmint, were there a thousand other, what did you call it, "womp-rats" armed with power rifles firing up at you?

'With all that firepower on the station directed at us, this will take a little more than barnyard marksmanship, believe me.'

Dodonna indicated a string of lights on the ever-changing schematic. 'Take special note of these emplacements. There's a heavy concentration of firepower on the latitudinal axes, as well as several dense circumpolar clusters.

'Also, their field generators will probably create a lot of distortion, especially in and around the trench. I figure that manoeuvrability in that sector will be less than point three.' This produced more murmurs and groans from the assembly.

'Remember,' the General went on, 'you must achieve a direct hit. Yellow squadron will cover for Red on the first run. Green will cover Blue on the second. Any questions?'

A muted buzz filled the room. One man stood, lean and handsome. 'What if both runs fail? What happens after that?'

Dodonna smiled tightly. 'There won't be any "after that".' The man nodded slowly, understandingly, and sat down. 'Anyone else?' Silence now, pregnant with expectation.

'Then man your ships, and may the force be with you.'

Elevators hummed busily, lifting more and more deadly shapes from buried depths to the staging area in the primary temple hangar as Luke, Threepio, and Artoo Detoo walked towards the hangar entrance.

Solo and Chewbacca were loading a pile of small strongboxes on to an armoured landspeeder. They were completely absorbed with this activity, ignoring the preparations going on all around them.

Solo glanced up briefly as Luke and the robots approached, then returned to his loading.

'You got your reward,' Luke finally observed, indicating the boxes.

Solo nodded once. He eyed Luke appraisingly. 'You're pretty good in a scrap, kid. Why don't you come with us? I could use you.'

The mercenary gleam in Solo's eyes made Luke mad. 'Why don't you look around you and see something besides yourself for a change? You know what's going to happen here, what they're up against. They could use a good pilot. But you're turning your back on them.'

Solo didn't appear upset at Luke's tirade. 'What good's a reward if you're not around to spend it? Attacking that battle station isn't my idea of courage – more like suicide.'

130

'Yeah . . . Take care of yourself, Han,' Luke said quietly, turning to leave.

Solo returned to his work, lifted a box – and stopped, to see Chewbacca gazing fixedly at him.

'What are you staring at, gruesome? I know what I'm doing. Get back to work!'

Slowly, still eyeing his partner, the Wookiee returned to the task of loading the heavy crates.

Sorrowful thoughts of Solo vanished when Luke saw the petite, slim figure standing by his ship – the ship he had been granted.

'Are you sure this is what you want?' Princess Leia asked him. 'It could be a deadly reward.'

'More than anything.'

'Then what's wrong?'

Luke shrugged. 'It's Han. I thought he'd change his mind. I thought he'd join us.'

'A man must follow his own path,' she told him, sounding now like a Senator. 'Han Solo's priorities differ from ours. I wish it were otherwise, but I can't find it in my heart to condemn him.' She stood on tiptoes, gave him a quick, almost embarrassed kiss, and turned to go. 'May the force be with you.'

'I only wish,' Luke murmured to himself as he started back to his ship, 'Ben were here.'

So intent was he on thoughts of Kenobi, that he didn't notice the larger figure which tightly locked on to his arm. He turned in astonishment as he recognised the figure.

'Luke!' the slightly older man exclaimed. 'I don't believe it! How'd you get here? Are you going out with us?'

'Biggs!' Luke embraced his friend warmly. 'Of course I'll be up there with you. Listen, have I got some stories to tell you . . .'

The steady whooping and laughing the two made was in marked contrast to the solemnity with which the other men and women in the hangar went about their business. The commotion attracted the attention of an older, war-worn man known to the younger pilots only as Blue Leader.

His face wrinkled with curiosity as he approached the two younger men.

'Aren't you Luke Skywalker? Have you been checked out on the Incom T-65?'

'Sir,' Biggs put in before his friend could reply, 'Luke's the best bush pilot in the outer-rim territories.'

The older man patted Luke reassuringly on the back. 'Something to be proud of.' He paused a moment before going on. 'I met your father once when I was a boy, Luke. He was a great pilot. If you've got half your father's skill, you'll do a damn sight better than all right.'

'Thank you, sir, I'll try.'

'There's not much difference control-wise between an X-wing T-65,' Blue Leader went on, 'and a skyhopper.' His smile turned ferocious. 'Except the payload's of a somewhat different nature.' He left them and hurried towards his own ship.

'I've got to get aboard my own boat, Luke. Listen, you'll tell me your stories when we come back?'

'All right. I told you I'd make it here someday, Biggs.'

'You did.' His friend was moving towards a cluster of waiting fighters, adjusting his flight suit. 'It's going to be like old times, Luke. We're a couple of shooting stars that can't be stopped!'

Once more Luke turned towards his ship, admiring its deadly lines. Despite Blue Leader's assurances, it didn't look much like an Incom skyhopper. Artoo Detoo was being snuggled into the R-2 socket behind the fighter cockpit. A forlorn metal figure stood below, watching the operation and shuffling nervously about.

'Hold on tight,' See Threepio was cautioning the smaller robot. 'You've got to come back. If you don't come back, who am I going to have to yell at?'

Artoo beeped confidently down at his friend as Luke

mounted the cockpit entry. Farther down the hangar he saw Blue Leader already set in his acceleration chair and signalling to his ground crew. Another roar was added to the monstrous din filling the hangar as ship after ship activated its engines.

Slipping into the cockpit seat, Luke studied the various controls as ground attendants began wiring him via cords and umbilicals into the ship. His confidence increased steadily. The instrumentation was necessarily simplified and, as Blue Leader had indicated, much like his old skyhopper.

Something patted his helmet, and he glanced left to see the crew chief leaning close. He had to shout to be heard above the deafening howl of multiple engines. 'That R-2 unit of yours seems a little beat-up. Do you want a new one?'

Luke glanced briefly back at the secured 'droid before replying. Artoo Detoo looked like a permanent piece of the fighter.

'Not on your life. That 'droid and I have been through a lot together. All secure, Artoo?' The 'droid replied with a reassuring beep.

As the ground chief jumped clear, Luke commenced the final checkout of all instruments. It slowly occurred to him what he and the others were about to attempt. Something now bound him to every other man and woman in this hangar.

Something crackled in his helmet. In response, he touched a small lever. The ship began to roll forward, slowly but with increasing speed, toward the gaping mouth of the temple.

TWELVE

Leia Organa sat silently before the huge display screen on which Yavin and its moons were displayed. A large red dot moved steadily towards the fourth of those satellites.

Dodonna put a hand on her shoulder. 'The red represents the progress of the Imperial battle station as it moves deeper into Yavin's system.'

'Our ships are all away,' a Commander behind him declared.

Slowly assuming attack formations combining X- and Y-wing ships, the various fighters began to move outwards from the moon to meet the technologic executioner.

The man who had observed the byplay between Biggs and Luke now lowered his glare visor and adjusted his half-automatic, half-manual gunsights as he checked the ships to either side of him.

'Blue boys,' he addressed his intership pickup, 'this is Blue Leader. Adjust your selectors and check in. Approaching target at one point three . . . '

Ahead, the bright sphere began to glow with increasing brightness. It shone with an eerie metallic glow utterly unlike that of any natural satellite. As he watched the giant battle station make its way around the rim of Yavin, Blue Leader's thoughts travelled back over the years. All these terrors and agonies were represented by the single bloated feat of engineering they were approaching now.

'This is it, boys,' he said to the mike. 'All ships, stand by to lock S-foils in attack mode.'

One after another, from Luke and Biggs, Wedge and the other members of Blue assault squadron, the replies came back. 'Standing by . . . '

'Execute,' Blue Leader commanded.

The double wings on the X-wing fighters split apart, like narrow seeds. Each fighter now displayed four wings, its wing-mounted armament and quadruple engines now deployed for maximum firepower and manoeuvrability.

Ahead, the Imperial station continued to grow. Surface features became visible as each pilot recognised docking bays, broadcast antennae, and other man-made mountains and canyons.

As he neared that threatening black sphere for the second time, Luke's breathing grew faster. Automatic life-support machinery detected the respiratory shift and compensated properly.

Something began to buffet his ship, almost as if he were back in his skyhopper again, wrestling with the unpredictable winds of Tatooine. He experienced a bad moment of uncertainty until the calming voice of Blue Leader sounded in his ears.

'We're passing through their outer shields. Hold tight. Lock down freeze-floating controls and switch your own deflectors on, double front.'

The shaking and buffeting continued, worsened. Luke remained in control and followed orders. Then the turbulence was gone and the deathly cold peacefulness of space had returned.

'That's it, we're through,' Blue Leader told them quietly. 'Keep all channels silent until we're on top of them. It doesn't look like they're expecting much resistance.'

They were now near enough for Luke to be able to discern individual lights on its surface.

'Look at the size of that thing!' Wedge Antilles gasped over his open pickup.

'Cut the chatter, Blue Two,' Blue Leader ordered. 'Accelerate to attack velocity.'

Grim determination showed in Luke's expression as he flipped several switches above his head and began adjusting his computer target readout. Artoo Detoo

135

re-examined the nearing station and thought untrans-latable electronic thoughts.

Blue Leader compared the station with the location of their proposed target area. 'Red Leader,' he called towards the pickup, 'this is Blue Leader. We're in position; you can go right in. The exhaust shaft is farther to the north. We'll keep 'em busy down here.'

'We're starting for the target shaft now, Dutch. Stand by to take over if anything happens.'

'Check, Red Leader,' came the other's reply. 'We're going to cross their equatorial axis and try to draw their main fire. May the force be with you.'

From the approaching swarm, two squads of fighters broke clear. The X-wing ships dove directly for the bulge of the station, far below, while the Y-ships curved down and northwards over its surface.

Within the station, alarm sirens began a mournful, clangorous wail as slow-to-react personnel realised that the impregnable fortress was actually under organised attack. Admiral Motti and his tacticians had expected the rebels' resistance to be centred around a massive defence of the moon itself. They were completely un-prepared for an offensive response consisting of dozens of tiny snub ships.

Soldiers scrambled to man enormous defensive-weapons emplacements. Servodrivers thrummed as powerful motors aligned the huge devices for firing. Soon a web of annihilation began to envelop the station as energy weapons, electrical bolts, and explosive solids ripped out at the oncoming rebel craft.

'This is Blue Five,' Luke announced to his mike as he nose dived his ship in a radical attempt to confuse any electronic predictors below. The grey surface of the battle station streaked past his ports. 'I'm going in.'

'I'm right behind you, Blue Five,' a voice recognisable as Biggs's sounded in his ears.

The target in Luke's sights was as stable as that of the Imperial defenders was evasive. Bolts flew from the tiny vessel's weapons. One started a huge fire on the dim surface below, which would burn until the crew of the station could shut off the flow of air to the damaged section.

Luke's glee turned to terror as he realised he couldn't swerve his craft in time to avoid passing through the fireball of unknown composition.

Then he was through and clear, on the other side. A rapid check of his controls enabled him to relax. Passage through the intense heat had been insufficient to damage anything vital – though all four wings bore streaks of black, carbonised testimony to the nearness of his escape.

'You all right, Luke?' came Biggs's concerned query.

'I got a little toasted, but I'm O.K.'

'Blue Five,' warned the squadron leader, 'you'd better give yourself more lead time or you're going to destroy yourself as well as the Imperial construction.'

'Yes, sir. I've got the hang of it now. Like you said, it's not *exactly* like flying a skyhopper.'

Energy bolts and sun-bright beams continued to create a chromatic maze in the space above the station as the rebel fighters crisscrossed back and forth over its surface, firing at whatever looked like a decent target. Two of the tiny craft concentrated on a power terminal. It blew up, throwing lightning-sized electric arcs from the station's innards.

Inside, troopers, mechanicals, and equipment were blown in all directions by subsidiary explosions as the effects of the blast travelled back down various conduits and cables. Where the explosion had hulled the station, escaping atmosphere sucked helpless soldiers and 'droids out into a bottomless black tomb.

Moving from position to position, a figure of dark calm amid the chaos, was Darth Vader. A harried Commander rushed up to him and reported breathlessly.

'Lord Vader, we count at least thirty of them, of two types. They are so small and quick the fixed guns cannot follow them accurately. They continuously evade the predictors.'

'Get all Tie crews to their fighters. We'll have to go out after them and destroy them ship by ship.'

Within numerous hangars red lights began flashing and an insistent alarm started to ring. Ground crews worked frantically to ready ships as flight-suited Imperial pilots grabbed for helmets and packs.

'Luke,' requested Blue Leader as he skimmed smoothly through a rain of fire, 'let me know when you're off the block.'

'I'm on my way now.'

'Watch yourself,' the voice urged over the cockpit speaker. 'There's a lot of fire coming from the starboard side of that deflection tower.'

'I'm on it, don't worry,' Luke responded confidently. Putting his fighter into a twisting dive, he sliced once more across metal horizons. Antennae and small protruding emplacements burst into transistory flame as bolts from his wing tips struck with deadly accuracy.

He grinned as he pulled up and away from the surface as intense lines of energy passed through space recently vacated.

Biggs followed Luke on a similar run, even as Imperial pilots prepared to lift clear of the station. Within the many docking bays technical crews rushed hurriedly to unlock power cables and conclude desperate final checks.

More care was taken in preparing a particular craft nearest one of the bay ports, the one into which Darth Vader barely succeeded in squeezing his huge frame. Once set in the seat he slid a second set of eye shields across his face.

The atmosphere of the war room back in the temple was one of nervous expectancy. Occasional blinks and buzzes from the main battle screen sounded louder than the soft sussuration of hopeful people trying to reassure one another. Near a far corner of the mass of flickering lights a technician leaned a little closer to his own readouts before speaking into the pickup suspended near his mouth.

'Squad leaders – attention; squad leaders – attention! We've picked up a new set of signals from the other side of the station. Enemy fighters coming your way.'

Luke received the report at the same time as everyone else. He began hunting the sky for the predicted Imperial craft, his gaze dropping to his instrumentation. 'My scope's negative. I don't see anything.'

'Maintain visual scanning,' Blue Leader directed. 'With all this energy flying, they'll be on top of you before your scope can pick them up. Remember, they can jam every instrument on your ship except your eyes.'

Luke turned again, and this time saw an Imperial already pursuing an X-wing – an X-wing with a number Luke quickly recognised.

'Biggs!' he shouted. 'You've picked one up. On your tail . . . watch it!'

'I can't see it,' came his friend's panicked response. 'Where is he? I can't see it.'

Luke watched helplessly as Biggs's ship shot away from the station surface and out into clear space, closely followed by the Imperial. The enemy vessel fired steadily at him, each successive bolt seeming to pass a little closer to Biggs's hull.

'He's on me tight,' the voice sounded in Luke's cockpit. 'I can't shake him.'

Twisting, spinning, Biggs looped back towards the battle station, but the pilot trailing him was persistent and showed no sign of relinquishing pursuit.

'Hang on, Biggs,' Luke called, wrenching his ship around so steeply that straining gyros whined. 'I'm coming in.'

So absorbed in his pursuit of Biggs was the Imperial pilot that he didn't see Luke, who rotated his own ship, flipped out of the concealing grey below and dropped in behind him.

Electronic crosshairs lined up according to the computer-readout instructions, and Luke fired repeatedly. There was a small explosion in space.

'Got him!' Luke murmured.

'I've got one! I've got one!' came a less restrained cry of triumph over the open intercom. Luke identified the voice as belonging to a young pilot known as John D.

'Good shooting, Blue Six,' the squadron leader commented. Then he added quickly, 'Watch out, you've got one on your tail.'

Within the fighter's cockpit the gleeful smile on the young man's face vanished. Then something hit and the interior of the now open cockpit became a mass of flames.

Far above and to one side Blue Leader saw John D.'s ship expand in a fiery ball.

On the fourth moon of Yavin a spacious screen chose that moment to flicker and die, much as John D. had. Worried technicians began rushing in all directions. One turned a drawn face to Leia, the expectant Commanders, and one tall, bronzed robot.

'The high-band receiver has failed. It will take some time to fix . . .'

'Do the best you can,' Leia snapped. 'Switch to audio only.'

In seconds the room was filled with the sounds of distant battle, interspersed with the voices of those involved.

'Tighten it up, Blue Two, tighten it up,' Blue Leader was saying. 'Watch those towers.'

'Heavy fire, Boss,' came the voice of Wedge Antilles, 'twenty-three degrees.'

'I see it. Pull in, pull in. We're picking up some interference.'

'Pull in, Blue Five. Pull in.' A pause, then, 'Luke, do you read me? Luke?'

'I'm all right, Chief,' came Luke's reply. 'I've got a target. I'm going to check it out.'

'There's too much action down there, Luke,' Biggs told him. 'Get out. Do you read me, Luke? Pull out.'

'Break off, Luke,' ordered the deeper tones of Blue

Leader. 'Blue Two, can you see Blue Five?'

'Negative,' Wedge replied quickly. 'Blue Five, where are you? Luke, are you all right?'

'He's gone,' Biggs started to report. Then his voice rose. 'No, wait . . . there he is!'

Relief swept the war room, and it was most noticeable in the face of the slightest, most beautiful Senator present.

Luke skimmed daringly low over the station's surface, his attention riveted on a distant metal projection.

'Stick close, Blue Five,' the squadron commander directed him. 'Where are you going?'

'I've picked up what looks like a lateral stabiliser,' Luke replied. 'I'm going to try for it.'

'Watch yourself, Blue Five. Heavy fire in your area.'

Luke ignored the warning as he headed the fighter straight towards the oddly shaped protuberance. His determination was rewarded when, after saturating it with fire, he saw it erupt in a spectacular ball of super-hot gas.

'Got it!' he exclaimed. 'Continuing south for another one.'

Within the rebel temple-fortress, Leia listened intently. Finally she turned to Threepio and muttered, 'Why is Luke taking so many chances?' The tall 'droid didn't reply.

'Watch your back, Luke,' Biggs's voice sounded over the speakers. 'Fighters above you, coming in.'

Leia strained to hear. She wasn't alone. 'Help him, Artoo,' Threepio was whispering to himself.

Luke spotted the object of Biggs's concern close on his tail. He pulled up and away from the station surface, abandoning his target. His tormentor continued closing on him.

'I can't shake him,' he reported.

Something cut across the sky towards both ships. 'I'm on him, Luke,' shouted Wedge Antilles. 'Hold on.'

Wedge's gunnery was precise, and the Tie fighter vanished brightly shortly thereafter.

It was comparatively quiet near the pole of the battle station. So intense and vicious had been Blue and Green squadron's assault on the equator that Imperial resistance had concentrated there. Red Leader surveyed the false peace, knowing it wouldn't last for long.

'Blue Leader,' he announced into his mike. 'We're starting our attack run. The exhaust port is located and marked. No flak, no enemy fighters up here – yet. Looks like we'll get at least one smooth run at it.'

'I copy, Red Leader,' the voice of his counterpart responded. 'We'll try to keep them busy down here.'

Three Y-wing fighters dropped out of the stars, diving towards the battle-section surface. At the last possible minute they swerved to dip into a deep artificial canyon, one of many streaking the northern pole of the Death Star. Metal ramparts raced past on three sides of them.

Imperial crews lining the trench rudely awoke to the fact that their section of the station was coming under attack. They reacted speedily, and soon energy bolts were racing at the attacking ships in a steadily increasing volume. Occasionally one would explode near one of the onrushing Y-wings, jostling it without real damage.

'A little aggressive, aren't they,' Red Two reported over his mike.

Unexpectedly, all defensive fire from the surrounding emplacements ceased. An eerie quiet clung to the trench as the surface continued to blur past the skimming Y-wings.

'What's this?' Red Two blurted, looking around worriedly. 'They stopped. Why?'

'I don't like it,' growled Red Leader. But there was nothing to confuse their approach now, no energy bolts to avoid.

It was Red Five who was first to properly evaluate this aberration on the enemy's part. 'Stabilise your rear deflectors now. Watch for enemy fighters.'

'You pinned it,' Red Leader admitted, studying a readout. 'Here they come. Three marks at two-ten.'

His screen revealed three Tie fighters in precision formation diving almost vertically down towards them.

'Three-eight-one-oh-four,' Darth Vader announced as he calmly adjusted his controls. 'I'll take them myself. Cover me.'

Red Two was the first to die, the young pilot never knowing what hit him. Despite his experience, Red Leader was on the verge of panic when he saw his wingman dissolve in flame.

Above them, Vader permitted himself a moment of pleasure as he readjusted his targeting 'puter. The rebel craft continued to travel a straight, unevasive course. Again Vader touched finger to fire control.

Something screeched in Red Leader's helmet, and fire started to consume his instrumentation. 'It's no good,' he yelled into his pickup, 'I'm hit. I'm hit . . . ! '

A second Y-wing exploded in a ball of vaporised metal, scattering a few solid shards of debris across the trench. This second loss proved too much for Red Five to take. He manipulated controls, and his ship commenced rising in a slow curve out of the trench. Behind him, the lead Imperial fighter moved to follow.

'Red Five to Blue Leader,' he reported. 'Aborting run under heavy fire. Tie fighters dropped on us out of nowhere. I can't – wait – '

Astern, a silent, remorseless enemy was touching a deadly button once more. The first bolts struck just as Red Five had risen high enough to commence evasive action. But he had pulled clear a few seconds too late.

One energy beam seared his port engine, igniting gas within. The engine blew apart, taking controls and stabilising elements with it. Unable to compensate, the out-of-control Y-wing began a long, graceful plunge towards the station surface.

Blue Leader tried to shunt aside the death of his old friend. 'Blue boys, this is Blue Leader. Rendezvous at mark six point one. All wings report in.'

'Blue Leader, this is Blue Ten. I copy.'

'Blue Two here,' Wedge acknowledged. 'Coming towards you, Blue Leader.'

Luke was waiting his turn to report when something beeped on his control board. A glance backward confirmed the electronic warning as he spotted an Imperial fighter slipping in behind him.

'This is Blue Five,' he declared. 'I have a problem here. Be right with you.'

He sent his ship into a steep dive towards the metal surface, then cut sharply up to avoid a burst of defensive fire from emplacements below. Neither manoeuvre shook his pursuit.

'I see you, Luke,' came a reassuring call from Biggs. 'Stay with it.'

Luke looked above, below, and to the sides, but there was no sign of his friend. Meanwhile, energy bolts from his trailing assailant were passing uncomfortably close.

'Blast it, Biggs, where are you?'

Something appeared, not to the sides or behind, but almost directly in front of him. It was bright and moving incredibly fast, and then it was firing just above him. Taken completely by surprise, the Imperial fighter came apart just as its pilot realised what had happened.

Luke turned for the rendezvous mark as Biggs shot past overhead. 'Good move, Biggs. Fooled me, too.'

Back alongside Yavin's indifferent bulk, Dodonna finished an intense discussion with several of his principal advisors, then moved to the long-range transmitter.

'Blue Leader, this is Base One. Double-check your own attack prior to commencement. Have your wingmen hold back and cover for you. Keep half your group out of range to make the next run.'

'Copy, Base One,' the response came. 'Blue Ten, Blue Twelve, join with me.'

Two ships levelled off to flank the squadron commander. Blue Leader checked them out. Satisfied that they were positioned properly for the attack run, he set the group to follow in case they should fail.

'Blue Five, this is Blue Leader. Luke, take Blue Two and Three with you. Hold up here out of their fire and wait for my signal to start your own run.'

'Copy, Blue Leader,' Luke acknowledged. Together, the three fighters assumed a tight formation high above the firelight still raging between other rebel craft of Green and Yellow squadrons and the Imperial gunners below.

The horizon flip-flopped ahead of Blue Leader as he commenced his approach to the station surface. 'Blue Ten, Blue Twelve, stay back until we spot those fighters, then cover me.'

All three X-wings reached the surface, levelled off, then arced into the trench. His wingmen dropped farther and farther behind until Blue Leader was seemingly alone in the vast grey chasm.

No defensive fire greeted him as he raced towards the distant target. 'This doesn't look right,' he found himself muttering.

Blue Ten sounded equally concerned. 'You should be able to pick up the target by now.'

'I know. I think my instruments are off. Is this the right trench?'

Suddenly, intense streaks of light began to shoot close by as the trench defences opened up. Near misses shook the attackers. At the far end of the trench a huge tower vomited enormous amounts of energy at the nearing ships.

Abruptly the energy bolts ceased. 'This is it,' Blue Leader announced, trying to locate the attack from above. 'Keep your eyes open for those fighters.'

Luke's attention was riveted to the surface of the station. 'No sign of – Wait!' Three rapidly moving points of light caught his eye. 'There they are. Coming in point three five.'

Blue Ten turned. Sun bounced off stabilising fins as the Tie fighters looped downward. 'I see them.'

Blue Leader adjusted his targeting instrumentation, pulling the visor down over his eyes. 'I'm almost in range. Targets ready . . . coming up. Just hold them off me for a few seconds – keep 'em busy.'

But Darth Vader was already setting his own fire control as he dropped towards the trench. 'Close up the formation. I'll take them myself.'

Blue Twelve went first, both engines blown. Blue Ten slowed and accelerated, bobbed drunkenly, but could do little within the confines of those metal walls.

'I can't hold them long. You'd better fire while you can, Blue Leader – we're closing on you.'

The squadron commander was wholly absorbed in lining up two circles within his targeting visor. 'We're almost home. Steady, steady . . . '

Blue Ten glanced around frantically. 'They're right behind me!'

Blue Leader concentrated on tiny, abstract images. 'Almost there, almost there . . . ' he whispered. Then the two circles matched, turned red, and a steady buzzing sounded in his helmet. 'Torpedoes away, torpedoes away.'

Immediately after, Blue Ten let his own missiles loose. Both fighters pulled up sharply, just clearing the end of the trench as several explosions billowed in their wake.

'It's a hit! We've done it!' Blue Ten shouted hysterically.

Blue Leader's reply was thick with disappointment. 'No, we haven't. They didn't go in. They just exploded on the surface outside the shaft.'

They neglected to watch behind them. Three pursuing Imperial fighters continued up out of the fading light from the torpedo explosions. Blue Ten fell to Vader's precision fire, then the Dark Lord changed course to fall in behind the squadron commander.

'I'll take the last one,' he announced coldly. 'You two go back.'

Luke was trying to pick the assault team out of the glowing gases below when Blue Leader's voice sounded over the communicator.

'Blue Five, this is Blue Leader. Move into position, Luke. Start your attack run.'

'Are you all right?'

'They're on top of me – but I'll shake them.'

'Blue Five to Blue pack,' Luke ordered, 'let's go!' The three ships peeled off and plunged towards the trench sector.

Meanwhile Vader finally succeeded in hitting his quarry, a glancing bolt that started small, intense explosions in one engine. Its R-2 unit scrambled back towards the damaged wing and struggled to repair the crippled power plant.

Luke saw that Blue Leader was in trouble. 'We're right above you, Blue Leader,' he declared. 'Turn to point oh five, and we'll cover for you.'

'Negative, negative. Stay there and set up for your attack run.'

It was less than a minute before Blue Leader's gyrating X-wing ploughed into the surface of the station.

Luke watched the huge explosion below him, knowing its cause, sensing fully for the first time the helplessness of his situation. 'We just lost Blue Leader,' he murmured absently.

On Yavin four, Leia Organa rose from her chair and nervously began pacing the room. 'Can they go on?' she finally asked Dodonna.

The general replied with gentle resolve. 'They must.'

'But we've lost so *many*. Without Blue or Red Leader, how will they regroup?'

Dodonna was about to reply, but critical speech sounded over the speakers.

'Close it up, Wedge,' Luke was saying. 'Biggs, where are you?'

'Coming in right behind you.'

Wedge replied, 'Okay, Boss, we're in position.'

Dodonna's gaze went to Leia. He looked concerned.

The three X-wings moved close together high above the battle station's surface. Luke studied his instruments.

Someone's voice sounded in his ears. It was a familiar voice: calm, content, confident, and reassuring – a voice he had listened to intently on the desert of Tatooine and in the guts of the station below.

'Trust your feelings, Luke,' was all the Kenobi-like voice said.

Luke tapped his helmet, unsure whether he had heard anything or not.

'Wedge, Biggs, we're going in,' he told his wingmen. 'We'll go in full speed.'

'We'll stay far enough back to cover you,' Biggs declared.

At high speed the three slim fighters charged the glowing surface, pulling out *after* the last moment. Luke skimmed so close over the station hull that the tip of one wing grazed a protruding antenna, sending metal splinters flying. Instantly they were enveloped in a meshwork of energy bolts and explosive projectiles. It intensified as they dropped down into the trench.

'We seem to have upset them,' Biggs chortled.

Luke didn't offer an evaluation – he was too busy holding a course through the turbulence produced by exploding bolts. Then, as if on command, the defensive fire ceased. He glanced around and up for sign of the expected Tie fighters, but saw nothing.

His hand went to drop the targeting visor into position, and for just a moment he hesitated. Then he swung it down in front of his eyes. 'Watch yourselves,' he ordered his companions.

They rushed on, closing on the target every second. Wedge stared upward, and his gaze suddenly froze. 'Here they come – oh point three.'

Vader was setting his controls when one of his wingmen broke attack silence. 'They're making their approach too fast – they'll never get out in time.'

'Stay with them,' Vader commanded.

'They're going too fast to get a fix,' his other pilot announced.

Vader studied several readouts and found that his

sensors confirmed the other estimates. 'They'll still have to slow down before they reach that tower.'

Luke contemplated the view in his targeting visor. 'Almost home.' Seconds passed and the twin circlets achieved congruences. His finger convulsed on the firing control. 'Torpedoes away! Pull up, pull up.'

Two powerful explosions rocked the trench, striking harmlessly far to one side of the minute opening. Three Tie fighters shot out of the rapidly dissipating fireball, closing on the retreating rebels. 'Take them,' Vader ordered softly.

Luke detected the pursuit at the same time as his companions. 'Wedge, Biggs, split up – it's the only way we'll shake them.'

The three ships dropped towards the station, then abruptly raced off in three different directions. All three Tie fighters turned and followed Luke.

Vader fired on the crazily dodging ship, missed, and frowned to himself. 'The force is strong with this one. I'll take him myself.'

Luke darted between defensive towers and wove a tight path around projecting docking bays. A single remaining Tie fighter stayed close behind. An energy bolt nicked one wing, close by an engine. It started to spark irregularly, threateningly. Luke fought to compensate and retain full control.

Still trying to shake his persistent assailant, he dropped back into a trench again. 'I'm hit,' he announced, 'but not bad. Artoo, see what you can do with it.'

The tiny 'droid unlocked himself and moved to work on the damaged engine as energy bolts flashed by dangerously close.

Fire remained intense as Luke randomly changed direction and speed. A series of indicators on the control panel slowly changed colour; three vital gauges relaxed and returned to where they belonged.

'I think you've got it, Artoo,' Luke told him gratefully. 'Just try to lock it down so it can't work loose again.'

Artoo beeped in reply while Luke studied the whirling panorama behind and above them. 'I think we've lost those fighters, too. Blue group, this is Blue Five. Are you clear?' He manipulated several controls and the X-wing shot out of the trench, still followed by emplacement fire.

'I'm up here waiting, Boss,' Wedge announced from his position high above the station. 'I can't see you.'

'I'm on my way. Blue Three, are you clear? Biggs?'

'I've had some trouble,' his friend explained, 'but I think I lost him.'

Something showed again on Biggs's screen. A glance behind showed the Tie fighter that had been chasing him for the past several minutes dropping in once more behind him. He swung down towards the station again.

As Luke soared high above the station another X-wing swung close to him. He recognised Wedge's ship and began hunting around anxiously for his friend.

'Biggs, are you all right?' There was no sign of the other fighter. 'Wedge, do you see him anywhere?'

Within the transparent canopy of the fighter bobbing close by, a helmeted head shook slowly. 'Nothing,' Wedge told him over the communicator.

Luke looked around, worried, studied several instruments, then came to a decision. 'We can't wait; we've got to go now. I don't think he made it.'

'Hey, you guys,' a cheerful voice demanded to know, 'what are you waiting for?'

Luke turned sharply to see another ship racing past and slowing slightly ahead of him. 'Don't ever give up on old Biggs,' the intercom directed as the figure in the X-wing ahead looked back at them.

Within the central control room of the battle station, a harried officer rushed up to a figure studying the great battle screen and waved a handful of printouts at him.

'Sir, we've completed an analysis of their attack plan.

150

There is a danger. Should we break off the engagement or make plans to evacuate? Your ship is standing by.'

Governor Tarkin turned an incredulous gaze on the officer. 'Evacuate?' he roared. 'At our moment of triumph? We are about to destroy the last remnants of the Alliance, and you call for evacuation? Get out!'

Overwhelmed by the Governor's fury, the subdued officer turned and retreated from the room.

'We're going in,' Luke declared as he commenced his dive towards the surface. Wedge and Biggs followed just aft.

'Let's go – Luke,' a voice he had heard before sounded inside his head. It sounded as if the speaker were standing just behind him. But there was nothing.

Once more, energy bolts reached out for them, passing harmlessly on both sides as the surface of the battle station charged up into his face. But the defensive fire wasn't the cause of the renewed trembling Luke suddenly experienced.

He leaned towards the pickup. 'Artoo, those stabilising elements must have broken loose again. See if you can't lock it back down – I've got to have full control.'

Ignoring the bumpy ride, the energy beams and explosions lifting space around him, the little robot moved to repair the damage.

Additional, tireless explosions continued to buffet the three fighters as they dropped into the trench. Biggs and Wedge dropped behind to cover for Luke as he reached to pull down the targeting visor.

For the second time, the energy beams stopped as if on signal and he was barrelling down the trench un-challenged.

'Here we go again,' Wedge declared as he spotted three Imperial fighters dropping down on them.

Biggs and Wedge began crossing behind Luke, trying to draw the coming fire away from him and confuse their pursuers. One Tie fighter ignored the manoeuvres, continuing to gain inexorably on the rebel ships.

'Hurry, Luke,' Biggs called out as he wrenched his ship in time to narrowly avoid a powerful beam. 'They're coming in faster this time. We can't hold them much longer.'

With inhuman precision, Darth Vader depressed the fire control of his fighter again. A loud, desperate shout sounded over the speakers, blending into a final agonised scream of flesh and metal as Biggs's fighter burst into a billion glowing splinters that rained down on the bottom of the trench.

Wedge heard the explosion over his speakers and hunted frantically behind him for the trailing enemy ships. 'We lost Biggs,' he yelled towards his own pickup.

Luke didn't reply immediately. His eyes were watering, and he angrily wiped them clear. They were blurring his view of the targeting readout.

'We're a couple of shooting stars, Biggs,' he whispered huskily, 'and we'll never be stopped.' His ship rocked slightly from a near miss and he directed his words to his remaining wingman, biting down hard on the end of each sentence.

'Close it up, Wedge. You can't do any more good back there. Artoo, try to give me a little more power on our rear reflectors.'

The Artoo unit hurried to comply as Wedge pulled up alongside Luke's ship. The trailing Tie fighters also increased their speed.

'I'm on the leader,' Vader informed his soldiers. 'Take the other one.'

Luke flew just in front of Wedge, slightly to port side. Energy bolts from the pursuing Imperials began to streak close about them. Both men crossed each other's path repeatedly, striving to present as confusing a target as possible.

Wedge was fighting with his controls when several small flashes and sparks lit his control board. Somehow he managed to retain control of the ship.

'I've got a bad malfunction, Luke. I can't stay with you.'

152

'Okay, Wedge, get clear.'

Wedge mumbled a heartfelt 'Sorry' and peeled up out of the trench.

Vader, concentrating his attention on the one ship remaining before him, fired.

Luke didn't see the near-lethal explosion which burst close behind him. Nor did he have time to examine the smoking shell of twisted metal which now rode alongside one engine. The arms went limp on the little 'droid.

All three Tie fighters continued to chase the remaining X-wing down the trench. It was only a matter of moments before one of them caught the bobbing fighter with a crippling burst. Except now there were only two Imperials pursuing. The third had become an expanding cylinder of decomposing debris.

Vader's remaining wingman looked around in panic for the source of the attack. The same distortion fields that confused rebel instrumentation now did likewise to the two Tie fighters.

Only when the freighter fully eclipsed the sun forward did the new threat become visible. It was a Corellian transport, far larger than any fighter, and it was diving directly at the trench. But it didn't move precisely like a freighter, somehow.

Whoever was piloting that vehicle must have been out of his mind, the wingman decided. Wildly he adjusted controls in an attempt to avoid the anticipated collision. The freighter swept by just overhead, but in missing it the wingman slid too far to one side.

A small explosion followed as two huge fins of the paralleling Tie fighters intersected. Screaming uselessly into his pickup, the wingman fluttered towards the near trench wall. He never touched it, his ship erupting in flame before contact.

To the other side, Darth Vader's fighter began spinning helplessly. Unimpressed by the Dark Lord's desperate glower, various controls and instruments gave back readings which were brutally truthful. Completely out of control, the tiny ship continued spinning in the opposite direction from the destroyed wingman – out into the endless reaches of deep space.

Whoever was at the controls of the supple freighter was perhaps slightly touched, but fully in command nonetheless. It soared high above the trench, turning to run protectively above Luke.

'You're all clear now, kid,' a familiar voice informed him. 'Now blow this thing so we can all go home.'

This pep talk was followed by a reinforcing grunt which could only have been produced by a particularly large Wookiee.

Luke looked up through the canopy and smiled. But his smile faded as he turned back to the targeting visor. There was a tickling inside his head.

'Luke . . . trust me,' the tickle requested, forming words for the third time. He stared into the targeter. The emergency exhaust port was sliding towards the firing circle again, as it had once before – when he'd missed. He hesitated, but only briefly this time, then shoved the targeting screen aside. Closing his eyes, he appeared to mumble to himself. With the confidence of a blind man in familiar surroundings, Luke moved a thumb over several controls, then touched one.

He blinked and cleared his eyes. Had he been asleep? Looking around, he saw that he was out of the trench and shooting back into open space. A glance outside showed the familiar shape of Han Solo's ship shadowing him. Another, at the control board, indicated that he had released his remaining torpedoes, although he couldn't remember touching the firing stud.

The cockpit speakers were alive with excitement. 'You did it! You did it!' Wedge was shouting over and over. 'I think they went right in.'

'Good shot kid.' Solo complimented him, having to raise his voice to be heard over Chewbacca's unrestrained howling.

Distant, muted rumblings shook Luke's ship, an

omen of incipient success. He must have fired the torpedoes, mustn't he? Gradually he regained his composure.

'Glad . . . you were here to see it. Now let's get some distance between us and that thing before it goes. I hope Wedge was right.'

Several X-wings, Y-wings, and one battered-looking freighter accelerated away from the battle station, racing toward the distant curve of Yavin.

Behind them small flashes of fading light marked the receding station. Without warning, something appeared in the sky in place of it which was brighter than the glowing gas giant, brighter than its far-off sun. For a few seconds the eternal night became day. No one dared look directly at it. Not even multiple shields set on high could dim that awesome flare.

Space filled temporarily with trillions of microscopic metal fragments, propelled past the retreating ships by the liberated energy of a small artificial sun. The collapsed residue of the battle station would continue to consume itself for several days, forming for that brief span of time the most impressive tombstone in this corner of the cosmos.

THIRTEEN

A cheering, gleeful throng of technicians, mechanics, and other inhabitants of the Alliance headquarters swarmed around each fighter as it touched down and taxied into the temple hangar. Several of the other surviving pilots were waiting to greet Luke.

On the opposite side of the fighter, the crowd was far smaller and more restrained. It consisted of a couple of technicians and one tall, humanoid 'droid who watched worriedly as the humans mounted the scorched fighter and lifted a badly burned metal hulk from its back.

'Oh, my! Artoo?' Threepio pleaded, bending close to the carbonised robot. 'Can you hear me? Say something.' His unwinking gaze turned to one of the techs. 'You can repair him, can't you?'

'We'll do our best.' The man studied the vaporised metal, the dangling components. 'He's taken a terrible beating.'

'You must repair him! Sir, if any of my circuits or modules will help, I'll gladly donate them . . .'

They moved slowly away, oblivious to the noise and excitement around them. Between robots and the humans who repaired them there existed a very special relationship. Sometimes the dividing line between man and machine was more blurred than many would admit.

The centre of the carnival atmosphere was formed by three figures who battled to see who could compliment the others the most. When it came to congratulatory back-slapping, however, Chewbacca won by default. There was laughter as the Wookiee looked embarrassed at having nearly flattened Luke in his eagerness to greet him.

'I knew you'd come back,' Luke was shouting, 'I just knew it! I would've been nothing but dust if you hadn't sailed in like that, Han!'

Solo had lost none of his smug self-assurance. 'Well, I couldn't very well let a flying farm boy go up against that station all by himself.'

As they laughed, a lithe figure, robes flowing, rushed up to Luke in a very unsenatorial fashion. 'You did it, Luke, you did it!' Leia was shouting.

She fell into his arms and hugged him as he spun her around. Then she moved to Solo and repeated the embrace.

Suddenly awed by the adulation of the crowd, Luke turned away. He found his gaze travelling upward. For a second he thought he heard something faintly like a gratified sigh, a relaxing of muscles a crazy old man had once performed in moments of pleasure.

For the first time in thousands of years that spacious chamber was full. Hundreds of rebel troops and technicians stood assembled on the old stone floor, gathered together for one last time before dispersing to new posts and distant homes.

At the far end of a long open aisle stood a vision gowned in formal white, barred with chalcedony waves – Leia Organa's signet of office.

Leia rose and came forward. All those gathered in the great hall turned to face the dais.

She placed something heavy and golden around Solo's neck, then Chewbacca's – having to strain to do so – and finally around Luke's. Then she made a signal to the crowd, and the rigid discipline dissolved as every man, woman, and mechanical present was permitted to give full vent to their feelings.

As he stood awash in the cheers and shouts, Luke found that his mind was neither on his possible future with the Alliance nor on the chance of travelling adventurously with Han Solo and Chewbacca. His full attention was occupied by the radiant Leia Organa.

She noticed his unabashed stare, but this time she only smiled.

THE SKATEBOARD BOOK

Ben Davidson

The skateboard is the sporting phenomenon of the
Seventies. Skateboarding parks, tracks and magazines
are mushrooming, outnumbered only by the millions of
fans who are taking to the boards all over the world.

And this is the book they've all been waiting for!
Lavishly illustrated with more than 70 photographs and
line drawings, Ben Davidson's manual presents the
art of skateboarding from a clear 'how-to' point
of view.

Technique, free-style tricks, safety, maintenance and
repair – these are just some of the topics covered in this
comprehensive skateboarders' guide. In fact, all you
need to know about our fastest growing sport!

GAMES & PASTIMES   95p

CLOSE-UP MAGIC

Harry Baron

The secrets of a professional magician!

Magicians, it seems, can perform the impossible. No matter how closely you watch, you'll find yourself baffled by their amazing feats. And when it happens right under your nose – before your very eyes – it's even more astounding!

Now, in this book, Magic Circle star Harry Baron reveals how these close-up stunts, puzzles, sleight-of-hand, vanishing and 'telepathic' tricks are done, and how you too can learn to perform hundreds more mini-miracles.

It doesn't need any special skills or expensive equipment – with Harry Baron's step-by-step instructions and just a little practice – you can mystify family and friends for a long time to come!

PASTIMES/HOBBIES

85p

All Sphere Books are available at your bookshop or newsagent, or can be ordered from the following address: Sphere Books, Cash Sales Department, P.O. Box 11, Falmouth, Cornwall.

Please send cheque or postal order (no currency), and allow 19p for postage and packing for the first book plus 9p per copy for each additional book ordered up to a maximum charge of 73p in U.K.

Customers in Eire and B.F.P.O. please allow 19p for postage and packing for the first book plus 9p per copy for the next 6 books, thereafter 3p per book.

Overseas customers please allow 20p for postage and packing for the first book and 10p per copy for each additional book.